"Go, Adam."

He drew in a short breath. "I—"

"Just go, Adam," she bit out, turning away from him so that he shouldn't see the sudden tears that welled up in her pained green eyes. "Please!"

He swallowed hard, gathering up his scattered clothes, not speaking again until he was once again fully dressed—and looking remotely approachable. "Andie, I—I don't know what to say," he began shakily.

"Then it's probably best that you say nothing," she told him tersely. Anything he said now could only make the situation worse. If that were possible!

"I don't know what happened," Adam said. "One minute we were furious with each other, the next—! I'm sorry, Andie."

Not as sorry as she was. Because, in the absence of the woman he really wanted, she had only been a substitute. But she knew as she looked at him that, despite everything, she still loved him!

Some women are *meant* to wed!

Meet the Summer sisters:
Harriet, Danielle and Andrea—
or Harrie, Danie and Andie,
as they're known to their friends!
All three are beautiful and successful,
though they've found their careers more
satisfying than relationships…. Until now!

Quinn, Jonas and Adam are about to cross
the sisters' paths. Harrie, Danie and Andie
find their hardworking, well-ordered lives
thrown into confusion. Even though they hadn't
been looking for love, each sister finds herself
wildly attracted! But will the exceptional men
they've fallen for pop The Question?

Find out the answer in Carole Mortimer's fast-
paced, emotionally gripping three-part series:

Harrie's story:
To Have a Husband
July 2001

Danie's story:
To Become a Bride
August 2001

Andie's story:
To Make a Marriage
September 2001

Carole Mortimer

TO MAKE A MARRIAGE

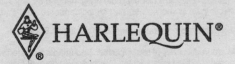

TORONTO • NEW YORK • LONDON
AMSTERDAM • PARIS • SYDNEY • HAMBURG
STOCKHOLM • ATHENS • TOKYO • MILAN • MADRID
PRAGUE • WARSAW • BUDAPEST • AUCKLAND

ISBN 0-373-12200-4

TO MAKE A MARRIAGE

First North American Publication 2001.

PROLOGUE

'TWICE a bridesmaid, never a bride,' he teased close to her scented earlobe.

The perfume of Andie, as he always thought of it. He had no idea what the name of the perfume was that she always wore, he just knew that whenever he smelt it, either on Andie or someone else, he was filled with warm thoughts of her...

She turned to face him now, a welcoming smile on her peach-coloured lips, green eyes glowing warmly as she reached up to kiss him in greeting.

Perfection. There was no other way to describe Andrea Summer. And today, in the frothy peach-coloured satin and lace of her bridesmaid's dress, with her long blonde hair a profusion of silky curls down the length of her spine, entwined with tiny peach-coloured tea-roses, she looked like a fairy-tale princess.

She laughed softly, a throatily husky laugh that sent shivers of pleasure down *his* spine. 'I think you'll find that it's "Three times a bridesmaid",' she corrected softly.

'It is?' he drawled with pretended ignorance. 'But you have to admit, your clock's ticking away, Andie; you're almost twenty-six now,' he continued mockingly, 'and both your older sisters have married in the last couple of months.'

She shrugged dismissively as she glanced over affectionately at those two sisters with their new husbands; the eldest, Harrie, had been married to Quinn McBride for sev-

5

eral weeks now, and this was Danie's wedding day to Jonas Noble.

'They have obviously found the right men for them,' Andie murmured fondly.

His own smile slipped for the fraction of a second, before he regained control. 'No "right man" for you yet, hmm, Andie?'

She laughed softly once again. 'I would have thought you, of all people would have known there's actually no such thing as the right person; it's all a case of taking pot luck!' she taunted contrarily.

Him, of all people…? Yes, he had always given the impression he was a confirmed bachelor; in fact, he had made a religion out of it! But this young woman—lovely to look at, always elegantly dressed, with a mischievously warm sense of humour—if she were only aware of it, could have changed all that with one crook of her little finger…!

How long had he felt that way about her? For ever, it seemed to him. Oh, there had been women in his life in the past, beautiful women, accomplished women, brunettes and redheads, as well as blondes, but none of them in any way had measured up to Andie.

'I hope you don't intend telling Harrie and Danie that!' He smiled.

Andie didn't return his smile. 'I don't happen to believe that's true for them; I'm as sure as they are that Quinn and Jonas are the right men for them.'

He was bored with the subject of Harrie and Danie; it was Andie he was interested in. It always had been. 'It's really good to see you here today,' he told her sincerely.

Andie frowned at the statement. 'I would hardly miss my own sister's wedding!'

'I can think of a couple of other family occasions you've missed this summer,' he persisted. 'The summer fête,' he added as she looked at him questioningly, referring to the fête held every June at Rome Summer's—Andie father's—estate. 'A family weekend at the estate a week later. Your father said that you had the flu.'

Andie shrugged, a smile playing about those peach-coloured lips. 'If that's what Daddy said, then that's what I had,' she dismissed. 'No mystery there.'

He took two glasses of champagne from a passing waiter; the wedding reception was being held at one of London's leading hotels. He held one of the glasses out to Andie, but was surprised when she shook her head and reached for a glass of orange juice instead. 'Don't tell me you've given up drinking champagne?' he exclaimed, knowing that in the past champagne was the only alcohol Andie had ever drunk.

'It's a new diet I'm trying out,' she dismissed, taking a sip of the juice.

'Diet?' He scowled, looking down at her already more than slender frame. 'You're far too thin as it is—'

'You're starting to sound like Rome now,' Andie taunted, blonde brows raised as she looked up at him from under thick dark lashes.

An irritated flush coloured the hardness of his cheeks. The last thing he wanted was to sound like her father, damn it! It was the very last thing he felt like whenever he was around her. Although, perhaps, to Andie, fourteen years his junior, that was exactly what he seemed...

'It's being featured in *Gloss* next month,' Andie continued lightly, referring to the monthly magazine of which she was senior editor. 'I thought I would try it and see if it really works.'

He scowled. 'You need to diet like—'

'You need to earn any more money?' she finished with

barbed sweetness. 'Have you never heard the phrase, "you can never be too rich or too thin"?'

His gaze narrowed thoughtfully at that slight edge to her tone. They had met briefly a couple of times during the last few months, never long enough to have a real conversation, as they were doing now, but he had been sure the flu excuse Rome had given him had been genuine and it hadn't been because Andie had been deliberately avoiding him. Now he wasn't so sure...

'I've heard it,' he grated. 'But I don't think you believe it any more than I do.'

'Really?' Her manner had definitely changed now, that hardness still there in her voice. 'We've known each other a long time, granted—but I don't think that gives you the right to tell me what I think!'

He reached out and grasped her arm. 'Andie—'

'I think you're going to have to excuse me,' she cut in firmly, having glanced across the room to where the bride and groom were now taking their seats at the top table in preparation for the start of the meal that was about to be served. 'It looks as if I'm needed.'

She was needed, all right. By him! He had felt this way about her since the day he'd looked at her, on her eighteenth birthday, and realised she was no longer an impish child but a beautiful, desirable woman. Almost eight years ago, he groaned inwardly.

His hold on her arm tightened. 'Andie, have dinner with me one evening next week,' he prompted forcefully.

She turned to look at him with cool green eyes. 'I don't think that's a good idea, do you?'

Good idea, be damned. This woman, it seemed, made him lose all sense of what was a good idea every time he came near her!

'I really do have to go,' she insisted, gently but firmly

removing her arm from his grasp before placing the half-drunk glass of juice in his now free hand. 'I hope you enjoy the rest of the wedding,' she added with banal politeness.

He had never enjoyed a wedding in his life, had determined long ago that he would never marry. But as he watched Andie walk gracefully across the room to take her place at the top table; he knew he would do anything to make Andie his own. Anything…

CHAPTER ONE

'I'M REALLY sorry to interrupt, Miss Summer, but there's someone outside to see you!'

Andie looked up with a frown, having been poring over a fashion layout that lay sprawled across the top of her desk. She had asked April not to disturb her for an hour, desperately trying to meet today's deadline, but as she looked at her secretary's expectantly flushed face her frown deepened.

'And who might that someone be, April?' she prompted dryly, knowing it had to be someone important—or April wouldn't have disturbed her at all.

April drew in a deep, excited breath. 'It's—'

'Adam Munroe,' the man himself announced with a smile as he strolled into the office, dressed as impeccably as usual, his charcoal-grey suit tailored across the width of his shoulders and the narrowness of his waist and thighs, his pale blue shirt made of silk, only the bright blue and yellow pattern of his tie giving any indication of the less than conservative nature that lurked beneath his outward appearance.

The arrival of Adam Munroe in the office was reason enough for April to have gone all aflutter, Andie allowed ruefully as she slowly put her marker pen down on the desk-top.

A long-time friend of her father's, Adam was a well-known film producer, but, with his tall, rugged good looks, and silver-blonde hair, he was gorgeous enough to have starred in one of the films he'd financed.

'Thank you, April,' Andie told her secretary dismissively, a slightly knowing smile playing about her lips as she watched April's slow retreat out of the room, the girl's avid gaze fixed on Adam the whole time.

Not that Andie could exactly blame April for that, either; Adam had been breaking female hearts with his charming elusiveness ever since she could remember. Elusive, because Adam always made it plain to the women he became involved with that the friendship would never lead to a permanent relationship. Not very romantic, but it certainly didn't seem to deter those women from becoming involved with him. In fact, the opposite!

Andie stood up slowly. 'After totally captivating my secretary so that I doubt I will get any more work out of her today—to what do I owe the honour of this visit, Adam?' she teased as she moved forward to kiss him lightly on the cheek.

He grinned, warm pale grey eyes surrounded by long dark lashes. 'I was just passing, and wondered if you would care to join me for lunch?'

She raised blonde brows. 'Isn't eleven-thirty in the morning a little early for lunch?' she queried.

He shrugged, making himself comfortable on the edge of her desk, disturbing several of the photographs that lay there in the process. 'Not when you haven't had any breakfast yet, no,' he observed pointedly.

Andie gave a wry smile, shaking her head. 'Hectic night again, hmm, Adam?' she taunted, moving back behind the desk to look up at him with mocking green eyes.

'Not particularly,' he replied dryly. 'I don't seem to be sleeping too well at the moment.'

'You—'

'Alone, that is,' he put in before she could complete her comment.

Andie chuckled. 'Maybe that's your problem; you obviously aren't used to it!'

'Very funny.' He scowled. 'The problem with you Summer sisters is that you have no respect for your elders!'

Andie held back her smile this time, although it lurked in the brightness of her eyes and the slight curve of her lips. 'Have Harrie and Danie been casting aspersions too?' She referred to her two older, now married, sisters.

Adam gave a grimace. 'When haven't the three of you teased me unmercifully?'

It was true, of course. But Andie and her sisters had known Adam, almost as an honorary uncle, for twenty years, and the fact that most women fell over themselves to meet him had been a constant source of amusement to the three of them as they'd been growing up. School friends, and then university friends, and eventually work friends, had constantly sought invitations to their father's home in the hope that Adam might be a guest at the same time.

'You know you love it, Adam,' she said.

'What I would love is some lunch.' He stood up. 'Going to keep me company?' He quirked blonde brows enquiringly.

'I'm very busy, Adam.' She gave a weary look at the layout on her desk.

'You still have to eat,' he persisted.

'Not at eleven-thirty in the morning, I don't!' she rejoined.

Adam gave an impatient sigh. 'I don't usually have this much trouble getting a woman to have lunch with me!'

Andie laughed throatily. 'A little denial is good for the soul!'

'It's *my* soul,' he returned. 'Please allow me to know what is and isn't good for it—and almost having to beg you to have lunch with me is not good for it!' he assured her scathingly.

If he weren't a mature self-assured man of almost forty, Andie would have said he had the look of a petulant little boy at that moment—one that couldn't get his own way!

She shook her head. 'You aren't begging, Adam. And I wouldn't allow you to, either,' she added seriously. 'But I'm not being deliberately difficult; I really am extremely busy.' She indicated the photographs scattered over her desk-top.

'Rome is of the opinion that you work too hard—and I have to agree with him when you can't even take the customary hour for lunch,' Adam told her, eyes narrowed on the slenderness of her frame in the silky plum-coloured trouser suit and pale cream blouse.

She had lost weight the last few months, Andie inwardly acknowledged. But she also knew it was a weight she would shortly regain. And more!

That thought sobered her somewhat, and looking up at Adam, 'Just when did you and my father have this cosy discussion concerning the amount of work I do or don't do?' she prompted.

'At Danie's wedding on Saturday,' Adam drawled challengingly. 'And there was nothing cosy—or underhand—about it; I merely remarked that you were looking at little pale, and Rome said that you're working too hard. That was the extent of our conversation concerning you,' he finished decisively.

'So you thought you would take pity on me today and invite me out to lunch.' Andie nodded, green eyes sparkling with anger now. 'It's very kind of you, Adam—'

'Don't get all polite on me, young lady,' he came back. 'For one thing—I wouldn't recognise you if you did! And for another—I'm not being in the least polite.'

'You just hate to eat alone,' she guessed.

Adam gave a reluctant smile, shaking his head as he raised his gaze exasperatedly to the ceiling. 'Either this used to be easier, or I'm just getting old!'

It wasn't either of those things, but she was busy—and, more to the point, she did not want to go out to lunch with Adam. Her life was complicated enough already at the moment, without that!

'It was a lovely wedding on Saturday, wasn't it?' She changed the subject—to one she knew he would find distasteful. Weddings and Adam Munroe just did not mix!

'Lovely,' he echoed with predictable sarcasm. 'First Harrie took the plunge, and then Danie on Saturday; I expect it will be your turn next!' he added disgustedly.

Andie looked down at her ringless left hand—knowing it would remain that way too. The man she loved, she just couldn't have...

'I doubt that very much,' she answered gruffly, blinking back sudden, unaccustomed tears. She had become so emotional lately! Definitely one of the symptoms of her condition that she wasn't too happy about. 'I'm destined to be an old maid, I'm afraid,' she explained self-derisively.

'Hey, I was only teasing.' Adam seemed to have seen that glitter of tears in her eyes, coming around the desk to put his arm about her narrow shoulders. 'There's plenty of time yet for you to fall in love and get married; you're only twenty-five, Andie—'

'Twenty-six in a couple of months' time,' she put in huskily, knowing he had completely misunderstood the reason for her emotion. It wasn't a question of falling in love and getting married; if she couldn't have the man she loved—which she most certainly couldn't!—then she wouldn't marry at all. Ever.

'That old, hmm?' Adam murmured softly, raising her chin to look into her face. 'Almost ancient, in fact.'

Andie shook her head, straightening away from him. 'You misunderstood the reason for my—emotion, I'm afraid, Adam,' she spoke firmly. 'I just find it very odd to realise that Harrie and Danie are no longer just my sisters, but are now Quinn and Jonas's wives.'

And she did find it strange. Three months ago none of the sisters had shown signs of marrying anyone, the three of them extremely close, so much so that they had never particularly needed other friends. And now to share not one of her sisters with a husband, but both of them, within the space of two months, was a little hard to take. Especially now...

Adam looked sympathetic. 'Harrie's the wife of a banker. And Danie—madcap Danie—' he shook his head a little dazedly 'is now the wife of a doctor. Amazing!'

It did take some adjusting to, Andie agreed. But there would be a lot more adjusting for Andie to do in her own life in the near future, than just to that of her sisters' marriages...

'Andie, come and have lunch with me?' Adam cajolled. 'If for no other reason than it will do wonders for my reputation to be seen with a very beautiful young woman!' he added encouragingly.

Andie looked sceptical. 'Another one?' she parried, knowing Adam had a succession of beautiful young women in his life.

He gave an irritated sigh, moving back impatiently. 'You know, I think Rome should have smacked your backside more when you were young enough to take notice!' He stood up.

'Mummy would never have let him.' Andie spoke confidently on behalf of her gentle-natured mother.

Adam sobered. 'True,' he agreed distractedly.

Andie knew the reason for that distraction. Had known it for some time. Adam had been in love with her mother…

He had been around a lot when Andie and her sisters had been children, appearing at the estate most weekends. Despite a dislike of the countryside and all things connected to it… It had only been as Andie had grown older that she'd realised the reason Adam had put aside his aversion and visited them anyway. Ten years ago her mother had died, and if the three sisters and their father had been heartbroken at the loss, then Adam had been inconsolable.

Because he had been in love with Barbara…!

Andie had been stunned by the realisation at the time, although it hadn't been a realisation she'd shared with her sisters, somehow finding the subject too difficult to discuss with her already distressed siblings. But she had wondered how her father would react, knowing Rome couldn't help but see the younger man's emotional state. Strangely enough Rome had seemed to draw comfort from the fact that Adam had loved Barbara too, an unbreakable bond developing between the two men, and now, ten years later, their friendship was stronger than ever.

Andie shot Adam a questioning look. 'Does this mean you've withdrawn your invitation to lunch?'

Adam looked crossly at her. 'No, it doesn't,' he snapped. 'And I'm no longer asking—I'm telling! Whatever that stuff is—' he waved an uninterested hand over the fashion layout she had been working on '—you'll deal with it much more efficiently once you've had something to eat.'

The fact that he was right didn't make the invitation any more palatable; she did not take kindly to being ordered about. By anyone!

She shook her head. 'The answer is still no, I'm afraid, Adam—'

'You aren't afraid at all,' he cut in harshly. 'Damn it, Andie, you and I used to be friends—'

'We still are,' she assured him coolly, completely unruffled by his loss of temper. Her father had a quiet way of doing the same thing when he couldn't get his own way, too... 'But as I've already stated—several times—I'm busy.'

'Fine,' Adam bit back, his jaw clenched. 'Perhaps I'll see if April wants to join me instead.'

Andie gave a grin. 'I have no doubt she would love to. But I'm also sure her fiancé would have a few things to say about it!'

Adam frowned darkly. 'You never used to be this difficult, Andie,' he said slowly.

She straightened in her high-backed chair, the sunshine coming in the window behind her giving her long hair the colour of ripe corn as it lay in a loose plait down her back, fine tendrils curling beside her ears and over her smooth brow.

'I never used to be a lot of things, Adam,' she told him tautly, the words tinged with an unhappiness she hoped he couldn't detect; the last thing she needed in her life at the moment was an over-curious Adam Munroe. It had been difficult enough, initially, to deal with an over-anxious Rome, without having Adam on her case now, too!

Adam looked appreciatively about the luxury of her executive office. 'You obviously enjoy being numero uno of *Gloss*,' he observed.

She gave an acknowledging inclination of her head. 'In the same way you enjoy running your own film production company,' she replied noncommittally, having the distinct feeling Adam was just making conversation now, delaying his departure for as long as he possibly could. Although why he should want to do that she couldn't imagine...

Adam gave her a considering look. 'Does that mean you've become a career woman, Andie?'

Not exactly! Especially as this was the last week she would be working on the magazine for some months to come. Which was another reason she was so determined to make sure everything was done perfectly for this, her final issue, for some time...

But despite the fact Adam was a close family friend, she had no intention of telling him any of that. Her nine months' leave of absence wasn't public knowledge, and she preferred that it remain that way!

'Not at all,' she dismissed lightly. 'Will you be coming down to the estate this weekend?' she asked, her expression still deceptively noncommittal.

Grey eyes narrowed warily. 'Why?'

'No particular reason,' Andie said casually. 'I just thought I should warn you, if you were, that Rome is not in the best of moods at the moment.'

Which was definitely an understatement! Her sister Danie had promised a few weeks ago to do everything she could to distract their father's attention from Andie and her present dilemma, but as it turned out Danie hadn't needed to do that; Audrey, their father's assistant for the last twelve years, had managed to do that quite successfully for them!

'I didn't think he looked too happy on Saturday,' Adam said. 'But I put that down to the losing-a-daughter syndrome.'

Andie chuckled softly. 'Daddy has been trying to give us away for years!'

Adam grinned. 'I wouldn't put it quite like that. He wouldn't give any of you away to just anyone.'

'That's comforting to know,' Andie replied dryly—although she knew that was actually the case. Luckily for Harrie and Danie their father approved of their choice of husband—otherwise one or both of them would have had a battle on their hands!

'Rome just wants a grandson to whom he can pass his business empire,' Adam assured her knowingly.

Andie looked down unseeingly at the photographs on her desk-top. 'And if we should all produce daughters?' she prompted gruffly.

Adam laughed, seeming unaware of her distraction. 'Then you'll all just have to keep trying until that male heir materialises!'

'I'm sure Harrie and Danie will be thrilled to know that!' Andie gave a hollow laugh.

'Look on the bright side, Andie,' Adam drawled. 'Until you find a husband it isn't a problem that need bother you!'

How little he knew...!

She didn't look well, Adam decided concernedly. Oh, there was no doubting Andie was as beautiful as ever. That would never change. Apart from her blonde hair, which she had inherited from her father, she looked exactly like her mother. And Barbara had been the most beautiful woman he had ever known...

But he knew Rome was worried about Andie, and, after seeing her at the wedding on Saturday, Adam had to admit he felt the same way. Andie still looked good enough to eat, but there was an air of fragility about her now that he had never noticed before, and a haunted look to those deep green eyes.

'So I really can't tempt you, then? To come out to lunch with me,' he pressed as she looked at him beneath mockingly raised brows.

She sighed her impatience. 'I've already explained—'

'Several times,' he agreed tersely. 'Will *you* be at the estate this weekend?'

Now her expression became guarded. 'Why?'

It never used to be like this between them! He had always had a close friendship with all of the Summer sisters, and Andie, as the youngest, had been able to twist him around her little finger. But there was a barrier between them now—and it wasn't a situation he was particularly happy with.

'No particular reason,' he replied. 'But it's a fact that I have been invited down this weekend, and, if Rome is as bad-tempered as you say he is, it might be nice to have some happier company along!'

Andie gave a loud laugh. 'Ever the bluntly honest Adam!'

He grimaced. 'You wouldn't know me if I suddenly became all charming and polite!'

'True,' she acknowledged evenly. 'It might be interesting to see, though,' she added softly.

Was it his imagination, or was there a wistful note in her voice…?

Wishful thinking, Adam, he instantly told himself.

Although there didn't seem to be anyone in her life at the moment; Andie had attended the wedding alone on Saturday. But Adam knew there had been men in her life in the past, and to even imagine that she might have been nurturing a secret passion for him all these years was the height of stupidity on his part.

'So what's wrong with Rome?' he abruptly changed the subject.

Andie frowned as she obviously readjusted her thoughts to coincide with his. 'Audrey has handed in her notice.'

'*Audrey* has?' Adam gasped disbelievingly.

Because he *didn't* believe it. Audrey Archer had been Rome's personal assistant for so long now, had become part of the Summer family life, it was almost impossible to think of any of them without including Audrey in the equation.

Andie gave an unhappy grimace. 'We're all as surprised as you obviously are, Rome most of all—'

''Surprised isn't exactly the way I would have described my own reaction,' Adam said.

'No...?' Andie looked puzzled by his words.

Were all of the Summer family blind? Adam wondered impatiently. It had been obvious to him for years that the beautiful Audrey was in love with her employer. Just as it had also been obvious that, although Rome might be unaware of it, to all intents and purposes, apart from the physical side of things—which, Adam had decided long ago, was none of his business!—Audrey had been Rome's wife in everything but name for at least the last ten years!

Audrey went everywhere with Rome, had dedicated the last twelve years of her life to all of the Summer family, becoming a surrogate mother to the three girls after their mother had died ten years ago; what on earth could have prompted her decision to leave them all now...?

With blinding clarity Adam suddenly knew the answer to that, too. Audrey had lost hope, had given up any romantic dreams she might have had of Rome one day coming to realise he loved her too.

Adam, probably more than most people, knew exactly how painful it was to love someone in that hopeless way. To have to stand in the background and watch the person one loved as they lived out their life, possibly with someone else, because that love would never, could never, be returned.

But the saddest part of this situation was that Adam was sure Rome actually did love Audrey—he just didn't know that he did! Ten years ago Rome had been devastated by Barbara's death, hadn't even seen there were other women in the world in the two years that had followed. Since that time Adam knew the other man had confined his relationships to brief, meaningless affairs, never seeing the love, or the beautiful woman who had felt that love, that was right in front of his nose!

'And what are any of you doing to try and stop her going?' he bit out tersely.

Andie looked taken aback at his accusing tone. 'What can we do?' she said. 'We're all upset, naturally—'

'Oh, naturally!' Adam came back scornfully.

Her eyes blazed deeply green as she glared at him. 'But Audrey seems to have made up her mind,' she continued determinedly, 'and so—'

'Hell!' Adam butted in furiously. 'Are all of the Summer family so wrapped up in their own lives, their own feelings, that none of you can see what this must be doing to Audrey?'

Andie's cheeks were pale now. 'Aren't you being a little unfair, Adam—?'

'No, I'm not, damn it, not even a *little* bit!' His hands were clenched at his sides. 'But I can tell you now that you've helped make my mind up about going to the estate this weekend. I shall most certainly be there—if only to lend Audrey a shoulder to cry on!' he blazed angrily.

Andie's gaze was cold now as she looked across at him unblinkingly, although a nerve pulsed in her throat. 'I'm sure she'll be very grateful—'

'You know something, Andie, I came here today full of good intentions, hoped we could share an enjoyable lunch together,' he told her harshly. 'But after listening to this I don't have any appetite for food, either. For goodness' sake, Audrey is a part of your family!' he groaned protestingly.

As I am, he could have added. But didn't. Because if

Audrey, who had been closer to Rome than anyone else these last ten years, and a second mother to Harrie, Danie, and Andie, could be allowed to just leave their lives without protest, then what chance did he have of meaning anything more to any of them?

It was certainly a leveller. One that made him feel slightly sick...

Andie gave a deep sigh. 'I'm well aware of that, Adam,' she said. 'And I have tried talking to her—'

'Obviously with little result if she still intends leaving,' he rasped.

She eyed him suspiciously. 'Maybe you will have more success this weekend,' she said softly.

Adam's mouth set angrily. It wasn't just because of Audrey, he inwardly acknowledged, shaken beyond words at the way she was being allowed to fade out of the lives of the Summer family. Could he, ultimately, expect the same fate?

He had met Rome almost twenty years ago, a young man of nearly twenty himself, with big ideas, and no money to back them up. Rome had been very much a business gambler in those days, and for several years he had become Adam's financial backer, Adam eventually in a position to pay him back, while at the same time being self-supporting. The last fifteen years had undoubtedly been highly successful ones for Adam, so much so that his film production company was worth millions.

His unhappy beginnings had been put behind him. In fact, they were something he preferred never to think about. But as a result, having no family of his own to speak of, over the years he had come to feel as much part of the Summer family as Audrey must do, had always regarded Rome as the older brother he had never been privileged to have, and he had always looked on the three girls as indulged nieces. They were his family!

He had been a fool to think nothing would ever happen to change that...

'Maybe I will,' he agreed grimly. 'It's a sure fact someone has to try!'

Andie looked at him wordlessly for several long, tension-filled minutes, until finally she turned back to the work on her desk-top. 'Perhaps I'll see you there,' she muttered, once again picking up her marker pen.

'Perhaps you will,' he rejoined grimly, turning on his heel and walking purposefully to the door. But he paused before leaving and his hand on the door-handle, he inserted, 'If you can manage to drag yourself away from your own interests long enough!'

Those green eyes were hard as emeralds as she looked across at him. 'I'm sure that if you can I can,' she finally answered in freezing tones.

Adam shot her a glittering glance through narrowed lids before swinging the door open, closing it determinedly behind him as he left.

The pretty young secretary seated at the desk outside turned to give him a shy smile, and it took tremendous effort on Adam's part to eliminate his scowl for the few seconds it took to give her a smile in return, before leaving. After all, she hadn't done anything to annoy him.

Who was he really angry with? he asked himself as he strode outside in the sunshine.

Rome, for being so blind that he couldn't see the unselfish love right in front of his eyes? A love he was about to lose...

Or Andie for seeming so indifferent about Audrey's imminent departure?

Or was he just angry with himself?

The latter was probably the more truthful, he accepted. He had gone along for years believing nothing would ever change, that Rome, Audrey, and the three girls would be there, as they always had been.

But nothing had stayed the same. Harrie and Danie were both married now, with homes of their own. Audrey had decided it was time for her to leave the family. And Andie—Andie had become a stranger to him.

And self-pity, he decided determinedly, was not an option!

CHAPTER TWO

AUDREY gave a wistful smile. 'It's simply time for me to move on, Andie,' she lightly answered the latter's enquiry.

Andie hadn't meant to come to the estate at all this weekend, had felt she was going to need time on her own after her enforced leave of absence from the magazine had started yesterday. But annoyed as she might have felt at Adam's remarks earlier in the week, they had struck a chord, and she had decided she had to come down after all and talk to Audrey.

She had arrived at the estate the previous evening, but this was the first opportunity she had had to talk to Audrey on her own, Rome a glowering presence at the dinner table the evening before, but luckily out on estate business this morning.

Audrey looked as beautiful and composed as she usually did, the blue of her tailored dress a match for the colour of her eyes, her blonde hair loose about her shoulders. But there was also a sadness in those blue eyes Andie had never seen there before...

'But move on where?' she questioned now as the two women enjoyed a mid-morning cup of coffee together in the sun-lounge.

Audrey gave a laugh. 'I haven't exactly thought that far ahead yet,' she admitted.

Andie's eyes widened at the admission. 'You haven't...?' she said slowly. 'But I assumed—I thought you must have found yourself a better job?' She frowned her confusion.

Was it her imagination, or did Audrey's gaze suddenly become slightly evasive. And if so, why had it?

Could Adam be right, after all—damn him!—and there was more to Audrey's decision to leave than was at first apparent?

Audrey shrugged. 'I'm actually thinking of not getting another job for a while. I have quite a bit of money saved—after all, what do I have to spend it on?—and so, I thought I might travel, see some of the world.'

Andie didn't feel in the least reassured by this answer. 'But you travel with Daddy all the time...'

The other woman sighed. 'Travelling with Rome is nothing more than a series of business meetings. Most of the time I have no idea which country I'm in at any particular moment; boardrooms look the same the world over!'

This explanation sounded feasible enough, Andie decided. After all, Audrey was only in her early forties, still young enough to want to do some of the things that she might have dreamed of in her youth. And yet...

Adam had put these doubts into her mind, Andie realised irritably. After all, it was Audrey's life, and she must be allowed the freedom to do with it what she wanted. The same freedom Andie had recently insisted on in her own life...

'You never know,' Audrey added with a smile, 'I might just meet someone and have children of my own. I'm not too old yet, you know.'

'You most certainly aren't,' Adam remarked firmly as he strolled unannounced into the sun-lounge. 'And whoever he is, he'll be a lucky man!' he added warmly.

Andie had known Adam would be here this weekend—he had made that more than obvious on Monday!—but, nevertheless, she was rather nonplussed at having him walk in on her conversation with Audrey in this way.

It was also a little disconcerting to hear him talking to Audrey in this slightly flirtatious way, especially as she was still processing Audrey's remark through her own thoughts!

She was ashamed to admit she had never thought of Audrey in that particular way before, had always assumed the older woman was happy with her life and career. Or maybe Adam was right, and they had all just selfishly taken Audrey's presence here for granted all these years…!

But Audrey was quite right, too; at only forty-two, there was still time for her to have a family and home of her own.

From the warmly appreciative way Adam was looking at Audrey now, he was more than aware of the other woman's attraction. And why shouldn't he be? There were only just over two years' difference in their ages…

'Thank you for that kind remark, Adam,' Audrey told him warmly as she stood up to kiss him on the cheek.

'I'm not being kind, Audrey.' He looked down at her intensely. 'I'm stating a fact.'

'I thank you, anyway.' Audrey smiled up at him as she squeezed his arm. 'I'll just go and get another cup and you can join us for a coffee,' she said before disappearing out of the room.

The silence that followed her departure was stilted to say the least, Andie decided as she glanced across at Adam beneath long lashes.

He was dressed casually today, in a black silk shirt teamed with fitted black denims, having thrown his silver-grey jacket into one of the wicker chairs as he'd entered the sun-lounge a few minutes ago. He was looking tall and lithe, his slightly overlong silver-blonde hair brushing the collar of his shirt, a slender gold watch nestling in the golden hair of his right wrist.

Adam looked exactly what he was, Andie realised: a

highly successful businessman, and a very eligible bachelor!

His expression was guarded as he looked across at her. 'You decided to come down, after all,' he murmured distantly.

He was still angry, Andie realised. But by what right? Okay, so they had all been a bit unthinking where Audrey's resignation was concerned, but Adam had no idea of the circumstances of the last few weeks—and he would remain in ignorance as far as she was concerned! He had no right to judge what he didn't understand. Besides, she still stuck by her position that it wasn't for any of them to stand in the way of what Audrey had decided she wanted to do.

'Yes, as you can see,' she replied, sitting forward in her seat as she prepared to stand up. 'You'll have to excuse me, I'm afraid; I was just about to go over to the hothouse to check on Mummy's roses.'

Adam gave her a derisive glance. 'I'm sure they can continue to grow for the next ten minutes or so without your checking on them! Long enough for you to sit with me while I drink my coffee, at least.'

She drew in a sharp breath at his undoubted mockery. She and Adam seemed to have been at odds with each other just recently—and she couldn't say it was something she was very comfortable with.

'I'm sure they can,' she acknowledged softly as she remained seated. She was feeling slightly vulnerable since her leave-taking of the magazine yesterday, and certainly didn't feel up to another confrontation with Adam. 'Did you know that it was Jonas presenting Danie with a bunch of yellow roses, just like the ones Mummy loved to grow, that confirmed for Danie that she was in love with him?' she continued conversationally.

'No.' Adam smiled as he stretched his long length in the

chair opposite hers. 'Although that sounds like the unpredictable Danie we all know and love,' he went on affectionately. 'How do you feel about having a doctor in the family?'

Her aversion to anyone in the medical profession, since going into hospital at the age of five to have her tonsils out, had become a family joke. And as Adam had been almost part of that family for the last twenty years...

She retained her casual demeanour. 'He could come in useful, I suppose,' she answered flippantly.

Adam chuckled. 'I'm sure Jonas would be pleased to hear it!'

'He's an obstetrician, did you know?' Andie said.

'I think Rome did mention it.' Adam nodded. 'I wonder how on earth Danie ever met him?' he asked thoughtfully.

Andie knew exactly how her impulsively madcap sister had met the gorgeous Jonas Noble. But that was something else that wasn't for public knowledge. And in this particular case, Adam was definitely part of the public...

'Rome is out on the estate somewhere,' she very firmly changed the subject. 'But he shouldn't be too much longer.'

'I'm not complaining,' Adam drawled, smiling warmly as Audrey returned with the promised cup and saucer. 'What man would complain about having coffee with two beautiful women?'

'One beautiful woman, I'm afraid,' Audrey announced. 'The post has just arrived, so I'll have to leave the two of you for a while,' she told them regretfully.

'Shall I pour, or would you like to be Mother?' Adam invited sardonically, once he and Andie were alone once more.

Andie gave him a sharp glance, her hands clenched tightly on the arms of her chair as she felt her cheeks lose all their colour, breathing shallowly in her shock.

Did Adam know? Had her father, despite her request for privacy, confided her condition to this man, his best friend?

Because she was going to be 'Mother'—in six months, she was going to have a baby!

The realisation of her pregnancy nine weeks ago had come as a tremendous shock to her, one that she hadn't taken to too readily initially. After all, without the baby's father in her life, it was something that she would have to go through alone.

But four weeks ago there had been the scare that she could lose the baby, and from feeling in the depths of despair, not knowing quite what to do, she had suddenly realised how much she really wanted her child. So much so that she wasn't willing to do anything that might jeopardise the pregnancy going full-term. Which was why, on Jonas's advice, she had taken a nine-month leave of absence from her high-powered, time-demanding job...

Her family knew of her pregnancy, of course, as did Audrey, but they had all been sworn to secrecy. Had her father now broken that promise and confided in Adam...?

Andie looked at him searchingly, seeing only light-hearted enquiry in his expression as he didn't wait for her answer but poured the two cups of coffee himself, and started sipping the strong, milky brew unconcernedly.

No, he didn't know, Andie realised with a thankful sigh. There would be plenty of time for that later, once her pregnancy began to show.

Strangely, she had lost weight at the beginning of her term, but Jonas had assured her that was only because of the worry and strain she had initially put herself under, because of her uncertainties, and that eventually she would start to put that weight back on. If the tightness of her clothing about her waist was anything to go by, that was starting to happen now!

But not enough, she was relieved to realise, for Adam to be in the least suspicious that his sardonic remark was actually fact! She was glad about that; Adam was the very last person she wanted to know about her pregnancy.

Because although she knew Adam had always been in love with her mother, Andie—for her sins!—had always loved Adam. Oh, she had always known it was a pointless love, that her feelings would never be returned, but she couldn't help that, she loved Adam anyway. So his pity—or even worse, his scorn!—concerning her pregnancy, were not things she felt able to cope with on top of everything else…

Adam sipped the coffee without tasting it, his thoughts broodingly introspective. He had been pleased on his arrival to see Andie had come down this weekend after all—damn it, he was more than pleased! But it had become glaringly obvious during the last few minutes that the strain which he had sensed between them on Monday was still there. In fact, it was worse!

Hell!

He drew in a ragged breath. 'How is Rome this weekend?' His coffee finished, he relaxed back in his chair.

Andie grimaced. 'About the same.'

Considering Audrey—from the little Adam had heard of the two women's conversation when he'd arrived—was still intent on leaving, he wasn't in the least surprised by Andie's reply.

He shook his head. 'I suppose I'll have to have a chat with him,' he said reluctantly; ordinarily Rome was the most genial of men, but not when it came to interference in his personal life. And whether Rome realised it or not, Audrey was very much in his personal life!

Andie gave a rueful smile. 'He's extremely volatile at

the moment, so make sure you have your body armour on first! I only asked him to pass me the pepper at dinner last night, and he almost bit my head off,' she explained with a pained grimace.

Adam groaned. 'Maybe I should come and look at the roses with you before tackling Rome.' He thought of the confrontation he would no doubt have with the older man once he had said what he felt needed to be said on the subject of Audrey's resignation. 'Isn't there some sort of saying about stopping along the way to smell the roses...?' he wondered.

Andie laughed as she stood in one fluid movement. 'I think that applies to people who need to relax more—not someone who wants to avoid someone else!'

Adam looked up at her appreciatively. Her golden-coloured hair was loose today, falling silkily down her back, framing the loveliness of her face, a face dominated by those beautiful green eyes, her skin having attained a light golden tan from the summer months.

Yet as he continued to look at her he realised there was something different about her...

But as he stood up to accompany her out to the hothouse at the back of the house, where Barbara had spent so much of her time tending her beloved roses, he couldn't quite decide what it was.

The heady perfume of the beautiful blooms assailed them as they entered the heated greenhouse, bringing back vivid memories to Adam of the woman who had first grown and tended them. Barbara had been such a lovely woman, inside as well as out, and her death ten years ago, from cancer, had been yet another blow in Adam's life. He—

Now he knew what was different about Andie! Like her mother before her, Andie always looked perfect, her make-up in place, no matter what the time of day, her clothes always beautifully tailored. Andie's make-up was still perfect, but for once she wasn't wearing any of her designer label clothes. Instead, she had on a loose green shirt over fitted denims, the former so big it looked as if it could be one of Rome's cast-offs!

Not that Andie didn't look as gorgeous as always; in fact, the casual clothing gave her a more approachable appearance, Adam decided thoughtfully. He was just surprised at the change in her, that was all...

She paused in the act of dead-heading roses, turning as she seemed to sense his gaze on her, a slight blush colouring her cheeks as she looked at him—warily, it almost seemed to him...? Had their friendship really come to that?

Probably, he acknowledged with a regretful sigh for the easy camaraderie they had once shared. But what had he expected? Nothing stayed the same. The fact that Harrie and Danie were now both married was testament to that.

'I was just thinking how much like your mother you are.' He spoke quietly, knowing, with this newfound strain between them, that Andie would not welcome any comment he might make concerning her personal appearance.

Andie's expression changed from guarded to noncommittal. 'She would have approved of Harrie and Danie's choice of husbands,' she commented huskily.

Yes, she probably would. Barbara, like Rome, had adored all of her daughters, wanted only the best for them. From the little he had seen of Quinn and Jonas, he had a feeling Barbara would not have been disappointed.

But what about Andie—would Barbara have approved of her lifestyle...? Andie was a career woman, had been the senior editor of *Gloss* for three years now, and showed no signs of wanting to change that for a husband and family of her own.

Yes, Barbara would have approved, he decided; Barbara would approve of anything that made her daughters happy.

Besides, Harrie and Danie still had their respective careers, as well as their husbands!

'I'm—'

'So here you are, Adam,' Rome's rasped comment as he entered the greenhouse interrupted what Adam had been about to say. 'Audrey said you were around somewhere.'

Adam briefly studied the older man, and he did not like what he saw. Rome's boyish good looks—blonde-haired, blue-eyed—were still the same, but there was a look of strain about those eyes and his mouth, a hardness to the latter that boded ill for anyone who got in his way.

'And, as usual, she was right,' Adam returned lightly. 'How on earth are you going to manage without her, Rome?'

Rome glared at him through narrowed lids. 'No one is indispensable, Adam,' he responded coldly.

Adam raised blond brows. 'No employee, possibly,' he returned acidly. 'But I always thought of Audrey as being more than that,' he added challengingly, aware that Andie was listening to the verbal exchange with a pained expression.

But it had taken only one look at Rome's face, at the hard implacability of his expression, to realise that the friendly chat he had intended having with his longtime friend was out of the question; Rome looked as approachable as a wounded bull-elephant!

Rome gave a dismissive shrug of broad shoulders. 'Obviously Audrey had decided differently,' he rasped harshly. 'And, as I have learnt to my cost recently, there is absolutely no point in trying to stand in the way of a woman who has made up her own mind what she intends doing with her own life!'

The remark, Adam knew, could have been directed at Harrie and Danie as much as at Audrey, and their determination to marry the men of their choice with as little delay as possible. However, Adam sensed, rather than actually saw, Andie's reaction to her father's remark, could feel the tension emanating from her as she paused in her care of the roses.

Leading Adam to wonder about the decision concerning what *she* intended doing with her own life Andie could possibly have made recently for her to assume Rome's remark was actually directed at her…?

Seeing no immediate answer to his question in either Andie or Rome's faces, he turned his attention back to Audrey; he would try and talk to Andie later on in the weekend. Try—because that hadn't been too easy to do just recently!

'And what does Audrey intend doing with her life?' he prompted the other man.

'I have no idea,' Rome answered scathingly. 'I suggest you ask her that yourself.'

'Meaning that you haven't bothered?' Adam countered, his expression deliberately innocent as the other man scowled at him.

'Meaning that Audrey has made it more than plain that it's none of my damned business!' Rome snapped.

'Hmm,' Adam murmured thoughtfully.

'What, exactly, does that mean?' Rome challenged hardly.

'"Hmm"?' Adam repeated, realising he was provoking the other man but knowing he had no choice if he was to get anywhere in this conversation at all. 'I've always thought of it as a pretty noncommittal remark, myself.'

'Then why make it?' Rome grated disgustedly. 'You—'

'Daddy,' Andie interrupted softly. 'Aren't you being just

a little—aggressive to your guest?' she said, once she had Rome's full attention.

Rome looked far from pleased at the obvious rebuke. Adam couldn't say he was exactly overjoyed by it himself; since when had he been relegated to being Rome's guest...?

But he already knew the answer to that, he acknowledged heavily. He and Andie, although still polite to each other— overly so, Adam felt!—were no longer friends, that easy camaraderie they had once shared no longer there. He knew the reason for that all too well, and regretted it more than he could say! More than he had ever regretted anything else in his life!

'I can take a little aggression,' Adam assured Andie lightly; in fact, he would relish it. His relationship with all of the Summer family had changed over recent months, necessarily so with Harrie and Danie, now that they were both married. But he had a feeling that if he were to speak as plainly to Rome as he wished to concerning Audrey, then he might jeopardise his friendship with the older man to such a degree that it would be irretrievable. Which meant his visits here would be a thing of the past...

Did he really want that?

Of course he didn't! His friendship with the Summer family had been his anchor for more years than he cared to think about!

But he couldn't just stand by and watch Rome make the biggest mistake of his life, either. He, perhaps more than most people, knew what it was like to love a woman who was completely out of your reach. As Audrey would be to Rome if he should let her leave...

'Let's walk back to the house,' he suggested to Rome as he walked over to join the other man in the doorway. 'There are a few things I need to discuss with you anyway.'

'And I thought you just came down to visit with all of us,' Andie put in with hard derision. 'How silly of me!'

Adam glanced back at her, sighing heavily at the sparks in her eyes as they easily held his.

His own friendship with Andie, it seemed, was already irretrievable…

CHAPTER THREE

SHE didn't have too much of an appetite at the moment, Andie thought—her morning sickness seemed to start in the late afternoon and continue until she went to bed! But the strained silence around this dinner table certainly wasn't helping to improve that situation!

Adam and Rome didn't appear to be talking to each other—indeed, Rome wasn't particularly talking to any of them!—and any remarks that passed between Andie and Adam were politely strained. In fact, the only person who seemed to be talking naturally and easily, to everyone, was Audrey!

The older woman looked dazzlingly beautiful this evening, her knee-length black dress shot through with silver, her smile warm and charming, her manner as friendly as usual.

But Andie wasn't fooled for a minute by the other woman's charming ease, could still see that sadness in the deep blue of her eyes...

'I thought salmon was a favourite of yours?' Adam was the one to break the awkward silence, looking at Andie as she pushed the grilled fish around on her plate.

It had been—but as with so many other foods she had once liked, now the mere smell of it only seemed to increase her nausea! The thought of actually eating any of it was complete anathema to her...

She put down her knife and fork, giving up all effort to try and hide the uneaten fish under the salad—she obviously hadn't been succeeding, anyway! 'I'm really not very

39

hungry,' she dismissed. 'In fact, if you'll all excuse me, I think I may just disappear outside for some fresh air.' She didn't wait for their response, standing up to let herself out of the French doors into the garden, breathing the air in deeply, hoping to eliminate even the smell of the salmon from her already quivering senses.

'Not exactly a lot of fun in there, is it?'

Andie turned sharply at the sound of Adam's voice; his hair looking almost silver in the half-light of this late-summer evening. She hadn't realised he had followed her—and she couldn't say she was altogether pleased at the realisation now!

She gave a rueful shrug. 'Rome has been like this for days,' she replied, wishing Adam would go back into the dining-room and leave her alone. She might have made her decision concerning having the baby, but there were still a lot of things for her to think over, and that was something she couldn't do around Adam!

Adam strolled across the patio to join her where she stood against the metal balustrade that looked out over the gardens. 'I don't think I've exactly helped,' he admitted. 'I told him earlier that he must be a fool if he's seriously going to let Audrey just walk out of his life in this way,' he explained.

Andie raised her eyebrows. 'And you're still alive to tell the tale?' she responded mockingly, well aware of how volatile her father was at the moment; she wouldn't have even dared to broach the subject with him herself! Although obviously Adam felt no such qualms...

He seemed relaxed about it. 'And to have dinner. Although from the way Rome is stabbing at his food rather than eating it, I think he wishes the salmon were me!' he joked.

Andie giggled. 'So you just left poor Audrey to face his moodiness alone!'

Adam sobered, his gaze intent on the half-shadow of her face. 'I was concerned about you.'

She stiffened. 'Me?' she echoed sharply, a pulse beating erratically in her throat. 'Why on earth should you be concerned about me?'

He gave a slight shake of his head. 'I don't know... There's something different about you.'

She turned away, swallowing hard. She was sure her pregnancy still didn't show; her black silk trouser suit, with its mid-thigh-length jacket, completely hid the thickening of her waistline and slightly larger breasts.

The latter had been quite unexpected, and were a bonus as far as Andie was concerned; she had always thought herself lacking in that particular area!

So in what way was she 'different'...?

'That bad dose of flu took a lot out of me,' she excused.

Adam disagreed. 'It isn't just that. Andie—'

'Leave it, Adam,' she cut in sharply, sure she knew what he was about to say. She didn't want to hear it!

This man had been, and probably still was, in love with her mother, and, while she might be deeply in love with Adam herself, she was not willing to be a substitute for another woman—not even her own mother!

Adam turned, reaching out to lightly grasp her shoulders as he gently turned her to face him. 'I think we need to talk—'

Her eyes flashed deeply green in the moonlight. 'Why?' she challenged, her head held back proudly.

He looked grim. 'You know why, damn it!'

'I have no idea what you're talking about,' she returned. 'Now if you don't mind, I came out here to appreciate the peace and quiet—not to engage in a verbal fencing match with you!' She glared at him. 'Besides,' she added, 'we both know how much you hate all this clean country air!'

Adam came down to the estate most weekends when he wasn't busy elsewhere, but he had never made any secret of the fact that he simply did not understand the liking Rome and his family had for country life.

'I could grow to like it, if I had to,' he said quietly.

Her mouth tightened. 'There's absolutely no reason why you should,' she responded hardly. 'I think one of us should do the decent thing—and go back inside and rescue Audrey from my father's foul temper!'

Why didn't he just let her go? She cried inwardly. His grasp wasn't tight on her arms, and yet she still tingled from his touch, warmth spreading through the whole of her body, her legs starting to feel as if they couldn't support her weight.

She still turned to liquid gold at his merest touch? After all that had happened? Despite all the complications her baby was going to cause in her life? In spite of the fact that Adam would never—could never—return her feelings!

She gave a self-disgusted shake of her head. Adam was way beyond her reach—even more so now!—and always would be...

'I—' Adam abruptly broke off any reply he might have been going to make to her suggestion as the sound of shattering glass was clearly heard from the direction of the dining-room, quickly followed by the sound of raised voices.

Andie turned back in alarm towards the house. 'You don't suppose Rome has completely lost it, do you, and actually attacked Audrey?' She gasped even as she pulled away from Adam and ran back towards the French doors that led into the dining-room.

From the scene that met her eyes as she rushed back into

the room, Andie had a feeling it was probably more a case of the other way round!

Her father was alone in the room now, standing back from the table, the front of his white shirt and the black dinner jacket looking more than a little damp, a shattered wineglass on the table-top in front of where he had previously been seated.

'What the hell have you done to Audrey?' Adam demanded, obviously having assessed the situation in a couple of seconds—and drawn his own conclusions.

Rome turned to him with blazing blue eyes, the mature handsomeness of his face contorted with anger. 'I'm sure it hasn't escaped your notice,' he replied furiously, 'but I'm the one with white wine all over me!'

The situation wasn't in the least funny, Andie inwardly thought, realising that Audrey must have been severely provoked to have thrown a glass full of wine—the glass included, by the look of it!—all over Rome. But, for some reason, she had the distinct urge to laugh!

For one thing, Rome looked ridiculous, with wine still dripping from his chin onto his already sodden shirt. And, for another—she simply admired Audrey for having the guts to act on her instincts. Andie could think of a few people she wouldn't mind throwing wine over herself!

'I noticed,' Adam drawled dryly. 'But I also know Audrey well enough to realise she must have been provoked into such an action,' he opined hardly. 'So what did you do to her?' he repeated.

'Nothing,' Rome bit out harshly, dabbing at his wet shirt-front with one of the snowy white napkins now.

'Daddy!' Andie gasped reprovingly; she also knew Audrey well enough to realise Rome must have said or done something to elicit this response.

Her father glared across at her. 'Whose side are you on?' he accused angrily. 'I—'

'I'm not taking sides,' Andie cut in. 'But I think I know the two of you well enough to be sure Audrey would not simply have thrown a glass of wine over you without good reason!' she added assuredly.

'Then you are taking sides.' Rome straightened to his full height of six feet two, throwing the damp napkin down disgustedly on the table-top. 'I never thought I would see the day when one of my own daughters—'

'If I still had the violin you forced me to learn to play when I was younger, then I would play it now!' Andie cut across this attempted emotional pressure on her father's part. 'But as I don't, and as you don't seem in any hurry to enlighten us as to the reason for Audrey's outburst, I think I'll just go upstairs and see if Audrey will be any more forthcoming!'

'She's packing,' Rome muttered as Andie turned to leave.

Andie came to an abrupt halt, turning slowly back to look at her father disbelievingly. There was certainly nothing in the least funny about this situation now!

'She isn't going to work the rest of her notice,' Rome continued. 'She intends leaving right now.'

Andie slowly shook her head as she saw the implacability of her father's expression. 'And you aren't going to do anything to stop her?'

Rome thrust his chin out arrogantly. 'There's nothing I can do.'

'Adam's right,' Andie snapped scornfully. 'You are a fool!' She turned on her heel and marched purposefully from the room, hurrying up the stairs and along the hallway that led to the bedroom Audrey had occupied for the last ten years.

But Andie hesitated outside the door, not sure how to proceed. Her father was in the wrong, she was sure of it, but that didn't mean Audrey was going to be any more pleased to see her than she would have been had it been Rome himself who came knocking on her door! But she loved Audrey, all the sisters did, and, despite what Adam might have assumed to the contrary, there was no way she was going to just let the other woman walk out of their lives in this way.

She straightened her shoulders, giving a determined knock on the door.

'Go away,' came Audrey's abrupt response.

Andie turned the handle on the door, relieved to find it wasn't locked, entering the room to find herself confronted by Audrey holding a vase of flowers aloft in her hand as she stood poised ready to throw it at whoever came through the doorway.

'I come in peace!' Andie cried even as she held her hands up defensively.

Audrey gave a shaky sigh before placing the vase of freesias back on the dressing-table. 'I thought it might have been someone else,' she admitted.

Rome... Despite Audrey's having had the vase of flowers raised as another weapon to launch at him, Andie could see that Audrey was actually disappointed it wasn't him!

Andie closed the bedroom door behind her, taking in the open suitcase on the bed, the clothes thrown haphazardly inside. Audrey really was packing to leave!

She moved to sit on the edge of the bed, realising as she looked around just how much this room had become Audrey's over the years. The décor was blue and cream, family photographs adorned the table by the window, Audrey's own as well as ones of Harrie, Danie, and Andie as they were growing up; the pastels on the walls were to

Audrey's taste too. Audrey wasn't just leaving a job; this was her home!

'Audrey.' Andie spoke firmly as the other woman continued to throw her clothes into the suitcase. 'I asked you earlier today why you were leaving, and you mumbled something about it being time to move on—'

'I believe I spoke quite clearly,' Audrey rebuked—although she didn't meet Andie's questioning gaze.

'Maybe,' Andie acknowledged. 'But now I would like you to tell me the real reason—and please, don't insult my intelligence again with that mumbo-jumbo,' she continued as Audrey would have spoken. 'I'm pregnant, Audrey, not mentally deficient!'

Audrey paused in her trips backwards and forwards between the wardrobe and the suitcase. 'I never for one moment thought that you were.'

'Well?' Andie prompted.

The other woman seemed to crumple in front of her eyes, tears filling those deep blue eyes. Audrey completely lost the tight control she had had over her emotions as she began to cry in earnest.

Andie rushed over to gather the older woman in her arms, moved beyond words at this complete breakdown of defences. She loved Audrey, they all did, and to see her hurting in this way was unacceptable.

'Audrey, you have to tell me.' Andie moved back slightly to look at her. 'I promise you I won't tell a single soul,' she promised chokingly, close to tears herself now.

Audrey gave a tearful smile. 'Surely it's obvious, Andie; I'm in love with your father! I always have been. And I always will be!'

Andie blinked. She didn't know what explanation she had been expecting; an affair with a married man possibly, perhaps even-wildly!—a past tale of manslaughter that

Audrey could no longer live with, but it certainly hadn't been this...

'Oh, Andie...!' Audrey laughed mirthlessly at Andie's stunned expression as she moved away to reach for a tissue from the dressing-table, mopping up all trace of tears from her cheeks. 'You don't see any problem with that, do you?' she asked hesitantly.

Considering Andie knew she had loved Adam as hopelessly most of her own life...no!

But, as she also knew only too well, it hurt to love someone so helplessly, to spend hours in the company of him and know that love would never be returned.

Although after the way her father had been behaving since Audrey had given him her resignation, Andie wasn't sure that was completely true in this case...

Had Adam known all the time of Audrey's love for Rome? Was that the reason he was so angry with them all?

'Doesn't this prove what I said to you earlier, Rome?' Adam demanded harshly.

'That Audrey is in love with me?' Rome repeated, moving to the side-dresser to pour himself a glass of brandy from the decanter there. 'Hardly!' He looked down pointedly at the damp stickiness of his clothing before taking a large swallow of the fiery liquid.

Adam gave the older man a pitying glance. He loved Rome like the father he had never known, or perhaps—more acceptably to Rome!—like an older brother. But, at this moment, he could cheerfully have physically shaken the other man to help try and make him see sense. In his business life Rome knew no rivals, became master of every venture he went into, and yet on a personal level he couldn't see the love right in front of his nose!

'I don't remember Barbara ever throwing wine over me

in an effort to show her love for me,' Rome commented at Adam's continued silence.

'Barbara obviously had more subtle—ways, of showing you what an idiot you can be!' Adam replied.

'Thanks for nothing!' The older man scowled.

He looked so much like a disgruntled little boy in that moment that for some reason Adam began to see the funny side of this situation, his mouth twitching as he made an effort to hold back his humour—at the other man's expense. Rome definitely looked less than his usually suave self with the sticky wine all down his shirt-front, and as for the indignant expression on his face...!

Rome's gaze sharpened suspiciously as he looked at Adam through narrowed lids. 'You wouldn't happen to be laughing at me, would you?' he accused with slow deliberation.

The grin Adam had been trying to suppress suddenly refused to be held back any longer. In fact, it came out as more of a choked chuckle!

'Damn it, you *are* laughing at me!' Rome grated indignantly, slamming down his now empty glass. 'Would it be too much to ask,' he continued between gritted teeth as Adam began to chuckle in earnest now, 'that you share the reason for this—this childish humour?'

Adam couldn't help it; Rome's angry indignation, on top of everything else, was simply too much—and he burst into a loud shout of laughter. Rome was priceless. Absolutely priceless. The man was as much in love with Audrey as she was with him—and was fighting capitulation every inch of the way!

Why else had he been in such a foul mood ever since Audrey had handed in her notice? Why else had he been so insulting to the poor woman that she had resorted to throwing wine over him? Why else had Rome brought

Barbara into their conversation just now, if not as a defence against the love he felt for Audrey...?

The man was as head over heels in love with Audrey as she was with him—he was just terrified of admitting it. To the extent he was willing to let Audrey walk out of his life?

Adam sobered slightly. 'I was just thinking it's a pity it wasn't red wine Audrey threw at you—it would have had a much more dramatic effect visually. Very much like blood, in fact,' he added with relish.

Rome didn't return the humorous smile that accompanied that last statement as he looked at Adam thoughtfully. 'You have a warped sense of humour, Mr Munroe,' he said.

'And you, Mr Summer, have no sense of humour at all at the moment,' Adam came back uncaringly.

Rome looked down at his shirt-front, pulling the damp material away from his chest. 'This shirt is silk,' he complained.

Again Adam had to hold back his humour at the other man's expense. 'Just tell the dry cleaners you had the shakes and missed your mouth!'

'Very funny,' Rome rasped—but there was at last a responding vestige of a smile on his lips. 'I've a good mind to ask Audrey to pay for it to be cleaned!'

Adam grinned. 'And risk having the bottle thrown at you next time?'

Rome looked crestfallen. 'You know, I've known Audrey for twelve years now—and I had no idea she had such a violent temper!'

Adam looked surprised. 'All that suppressed passion has to be released somehow.'

Rome was nonplussed. 'And exactly what would you know about Audrey's suppressed passion?'

Adam moved to the drinks tray to pour them both a brandy, handing one of the glasses to the other man before making his reply. 'From the mood you've been in the last few weeks—about as much as you obviously do!'

Rome gave a heavy sigh as he sat down in one of the chairs set about the dining-table—not the one he had been sitting in earlier, because that was as damp as his shirt! 'Women!' he muttered with feeling.

'Not only a different species but from another planet as well,' Adam agreed as he joined the other man and sat back down at the table.

'Obviously one of far superior intellect!' Andie snapped as she swept into the room, looking like an enraged tigress as she came to stand at the other end of the table, green eyes flashing angrily as she glared at each man in turn.

Adam gave an inward groan; his remark had been meant to mock Rome, not be taken as an insult by a member of that different species from another planet! But it didn't need anyone of superior intellect to know that Andie definitely felt insulted!

Andie continued to look at the two men with disgust. 'While the two of you have been down here discussing women like a couple of immature boys after their first date, I have been upstairs trying to persuade Audrey that whatever you said to her—' she looked straight at her father '—you didn't mean. Not only that, I assured her that you will most certainly apologise to her for making the remark.'

'You—'

'I even talked her out of smashing a vase of flowers over your head as soon as you enter the room,' Andie added scathingly as Rome would have spoken.

Rome turned to Adam. 'I think I liked the red wine idea better,' he said consideringly. 'As you said, much more dramatic!'

Adam could see by the fury of Andie's expression that this was not the time for levity, and yet he couldn't help but smile at the other man's remark. At least Rome had got his sense of humour back!

Although the look on Andie's face as she saw his smile didn't augur well for her own humour!

'When the two of you have quite finished behaving like a couple of juvenile delinquents, I—'

'Immature *and* juvenile,' Rome amended with a considering tilt of his head. 'Not bad going for men of fifty-four and nearly forty!'

'At this moment three and four is probably nearer the mark!' Andie bit back before turning to her father with glittering green eyes. 'Rome, if you don't go upstairs and apologise to Audrey right now—'

'Yes?' Rome prompted softly at the threat in her tone, his own gaze narrowed warningly now.

Adam could see by the sudden flush to Andie's cheeks that she had heard that warning—but he also knew by the following stubborn set of her mouth that it was going to be a warning she ignored. He gave a pained wince as he waited for her response.

'You're going to lose her for good,' Andie stated baldly. 'And that's something you're going to regret for the rest of your life,' she declared with certainty.

Her words were nothing like Adam had thought they would be. Or Rome either, if the stunned look on his face was anything to go by!

'What is it with everyone this evening?' Rome implored as he stood up noisily. 'Suddenly you all know what's better for me than I do myself!' He began to pace the room, stopping every now and then to glare impatiently at either Andie or Adam, finally coming to a halt near the doorway. 'Well, I've listened to what the two of you have had to say this evening—maybe not patiently, but I've certainly listened. And do you want to know the biggest conclusion I've come to…?'

Adam had the distinct impression that he, for one, didn't want to know. But quickly following on the heels of that realisation was the fact that he wasn't going to have any choice in the matter!

'The conclusion I've come to is that the two of *you* should sort out your own lives before you start telling me what I should or shouldn't do with mine!' Rome told them bluntly.

Adam looked warily across at the other man, and, without so much as glancing at Andie, he could feel her sudden tension. What exactly, he wondered, did Rome mean by that remark…? More to the point, what was he going to say next?

Rome gave a humourless smile as he took in their stunned expressions. 'Not so pleasant when it's directed at you, is it?' he derided. 'For instance, Adam—' Rome turned to him '—it's way past time you stopped this carefree bachelor life, settled down with one of those beautiful women you're always seen parading around with, and raised your own family instead of sharing mine. And, as for you, Andie—'

'That's enough, Daddy,' she told him through stiff lips, her face very pale now, her hands clenched at her sides.

'But—'

'I said that was enough!' she burst out.

Rome gave another heavy sigh. 'Maybe it is,' he conceded evenly. 'Now if you'll both excuse me,' he said as the sound of the front door opening could be clearly heard, 'I have to go out there and persuade Audrey out of doing something I'm going to regret for the rest of my life!' The door closed decisively behind him as he left the room.

The silence he left behind him was so filled with tension Adam felt as if he might reach out and touch it.

But he certainly dared not reach out and touch Andie, he realised as he looked across at her. That barrier seemed to have fallen between them again; her expression was remote, her gaze, when it met his, cold...

'Well, I must say, I'm really impressed that the two of you found Audrey's behaviour so damned funny!' she finally burst out, eyes flashing deeply green.

The adage 'attack is the best form of defence' came unbidden to Adam's mind...

He had no idea why; after all, Andie's outburst was probably merited. Except... 'I didn't find it in the least funny,' Adam told her sharply. 'If you must know, I was trying to calm Rome down by making him see the funny side of it!'

Andie gave him a scornful look as the sound of raised voices could clearly be heard outside in the hallway. 'I don't think Audrey appreciates your efforts any more than I did! Sitting down here laughing about the situation like a couple of—'

'Schoolboys,' Adam finished for her, starting to feel angry himself now. Why did this woman always misinterpret what he was trying to say or do?

'Exactly.' She gave him another scathing glance. 'A "different species from another planet!"' she repeated.

'But with superior intellect,' he repeated dryly, striding forcefully across the room to lightly grasp the tops of her arms when he received no answering smile from Andie. 'You know, Andie, you've certainly lost *your* sense of humour the last few weeks,' he told her.

Andie looked up at him unsmilingly. 'Probably because I see very little to smile about the last few weeks,' she responded. 'Now, if you wouldn't mind releasing me...? I'm tired and would like to go to bed.'

Adam looked at her searchingly. She did look tired. But it wasn't just that. There was also that hardness about her eyes and mouth. And he could tell by the way she strained against his hold on her arms that she did not like him touching her... Had it really come to that, to a point where she couldn't even bear him to touch her?

'Don't you think we should let the lovebirds have a little more time to settle their differences?' he cajoled huskily, the sound of voices outside still audible in the dining-room.

'Would you please let me go?' Andie said through gritted teeth.

She really didn't like him touching her, Adam accepted heavily. Whereas he—he wanted to touch her, damn it. In fact, he wanted to do a lot more than just touch her!

Andie's gaze narrowed glitteringly as she seemed to read at least some of his thoughts from his expression. 'Don't even think about it, Adam,' she warned softly.

Perhaps it was that warning tone. Or perhaps his patience had been tried too far. Whatever the reason, he did a sight more than just think about it!

She felt curvaceously desirable, Adam briefly had time to register as he pulled her to him. But only briefly—because as his lips fused with hers he could think of nothing but that. Actually, he couldn't think at all, could only feel! Andie felt so good to him, her body curved into the hard contours of his, her hands tightly gripping his shoulders.

Now he knew how a thirsty man in a desert had to feel when offered water. He wanted to drink, and drink, and drink, never wanted this to stop!

But even as he recognised that, that was exactly what it did, Andie wrenching her mouth away from his, pushing at his chest until he had no choice but to release her.

She stood removed from him now, her head held back defiantly, her nostrils flaring angrily as she breathed deeply.

'That was a mistake on your part, Adam,' she said gratingly. 'And one definitely not to be repeated.' She pushed the blonde tumble of her hair back from her angrily flushed face.

Adam would have liked to throw her words back in her face, wished for nothing more than to be able to claim that she had responded. But the truth of the matter was, she hadn't. For several long—glorious!—seconds she had remained impassive in his arms—rather like a wooden doll?—and then she had begun to fight him.

He drew in a ragged breath, putting a hand up to a temple that suddenly ached with tension. 'Are we never going to be friends again, Andie?' he said dully.

'Friends!' she repeated harshly. 'I've always tried to be your friend, Adam, but it obviously isn't a friend that you want—'

'Tried?' he echoed incredulously feeling as if she had just punched him in the solar plexus.

'Tried,' she repeated firmly, the coldness of her gaze easily holding his. 'But I can't even do that any more, Adam,' she told him flatly. 'I suggest that in future we just try to stay out of each other's way.'

He swallowed hard, knowing by her implacable expression that she meant exactly what she had just said. But how could he stay away from her—when what he most wanted to do was the exact opposite to that?

No!

Much as he might want Andie, he certainly wasn't what Andie needed in her life.

'I think you're right, Andie,' he said shortly. 'You are tired and need to go to bed. We can talk about this again tomorrow.' When he had recovered sufficiently from this talk to be able to deal with the situation logically.

'My conclusion will be exactly the same, tomorrow or

any other day!' Andie snapped before sweeping from the room, leaving a trail of her heady perfume in her wake.

Adam almost fell into the chair, putting his hands up to cover his face as he gave a pained groan.

Andie had always tried to be his friend!

Until he had ruined even that...?

CHAPTER FOUR

'JUST how long did you think you could keep the existence of my child from me?'

Andie flinched at the sound of that angrily accusing voice, but she didn't open her eyes, or move from her prone position on the sun-lounger on the terrace of her father's Majorcan villa.

His child, he had said...

Yes, she was carrying his child. The baby was hers too, of course, but she knew him well enough to realise he wouldn't just stand by and ignore his own child.

Although, as he seemed to have guessed, that hadn't prevented Andie wanting to stop him from having that knowledge for as long as possible. Which was what she was doing in Majorca in the first place.

It had started out as a germ of an idea, a need for a complete—if temporary!—break, away from the emotional pressures being brought to bear concerning her pregnancy. With no magazine to go to each weekday, and her father's attention thankfully occupied elsewhere, it hadn't been too difficult to make the move to the Majorcan sunshine for a few weeks. To put off, for a short time longer, the confrontation that now seemed to have come to her...

How had she ever got herself into this mess?

Ah, yes...she remembered now. It had begun, quite innocently, with an invitation to attend a party as Adam Munroe's partner. She gave a rueful smile as she remembered teasing him about the unexpected invitation...

'Don't tell me the eligible Adam Munroe has been stood

up?' she taunted at the twenty-four hours' notice he had given her.

He shook his head unconcernedly. 'I was actually going to attend alone,' he drawled. 'But then I thought you might find it rather fun.'

'Run out of ambitious young actresses just longing to be seen on the arm of the influential film producer Adam Munroe?' Andie looked up from her desk to venture.

Adam grinned unabashedly, perched on the side of her desk. 'Tired of their unsubtle machinations,' he revealed. 'At least I know you don't have any ambitions to become an actress!'

Andie had to smile. 'Not the most charming invitation I've ever received!'

'But you'll come anyway?'

Why not? Her social calendar wasn't exactly overflowing with invitations. From choice, she acknowledged. No man, she had learnt through dating over the years, could in any way measure up to the man she was already in love with. The man who, for reasons of his own, was inviting her to spend tomorrow evening with him...

She looked up at Adam with searching eyes. What was it about this man that held her so enthralled? Oh, he was handsome enough, but then so were a lot of other men she had met. Adam could be incredibly charming too—but that wasn't unique, either. No, she had no idea why it should be this man she loved; she only knew that she did. That she always had.

And the temptation to spend an evening in his company was just too great to refuse...

'Okay, Adam,' she decided firmly—before she could have second thoughts about the prudence of going out with him at all. 'What time shall I be ready? And what do you want me to wear?'

'Eight o'clock.' He smiled his pleasure in her acquiescence. 'And I wouldn't presume to tell you what you should wear.'

Andie gave a wry smile. 'It's never stopped you before!' she clearly remembered one occasion, that of her eighteenth birthday, when Adam had been less than polite concerning the figure-hugging red dress she had been wearing!

He continued to grin. 'Maybe I'm getting more circumspect in my old age,' he drawled.

Andie quirked one mocking brow. 'I doubt that very much. Okay, Adam, I'll use my own judgement,' she assured him.

And she did, the knee-length shimmering silver dress clinging lovingly to every curve of her body, the low neckline revealing a tempting expanse of creamy breasts. Her blonde hair she left loose down the length of her spine, silver lights reflecting from the dress, her jewellery of chunky gold earrings and bracelet, giving her a delicacy that was refuted by the teasing mischief lurking in her deep green gaze.

Adam, she was pleased to note, was completely bowled over by her appearance when she opened her apartment door to him the following evening.

'May I say, Miss Summer, that you dress up quite spectacularly?' he told her.

'And may I say, Mr Munroe, that so do you?' she returned flirtatiously in an effort to hide her own reaction to his lethal handsomeness in the black dinner suit and snowy white shirt. Not that she could hide her reaction completely, conscious of a pulse beating erratically at the base of her creamy throat.

'Your carriage awaits, my lady.' He gave a theatrical sweep of his arm.

Her 'carriage' consisted of Adam's sleek green Jaguar

sports car. She showed a long expanse of slenderly silky leg as Adam held the door open for her to slip into the passenger seat.

She gave him a reproving look as he got into the car beside her, still trying to pull her dress down to a respectable level. 'I can't help thinking, Adam, that you chose such a low car deliberately!'

He quirked blond brows at her before turning the key in the ignition. 'Actually, Andie—I can't help thinking the same thing!' he returned unrepentantly.

Adam drove out of London towards Berkshire, their hosts for the evening turning out to be the Grants, the film director Daniel, and his beautiful actress wife Carla Burton, the latter heavily pregnant with their second child.

There wasn't a single guest at the party that Andie didn't recognise from either film or television, and, while her own highly indulged upbringing meant she wasn't in the least overwhelmed by so many celebrities, she couldn't say she was exactly overjoyed when, shortly after their arrival, Adam, having provided her with a glass of champagne, excused himself to go and talk to the latest darling of the film world, Elizabeth King.

In fact, Adam's attention on the beautiful redhead was so intense over the next ten minutes that Andie couldn't help wondering why on earth he had needed to bring her here with him at all!

'Actress or television presenter?' The teasing male voice at her side drew her attention away from Adam and the beautiful actress.

She turned to find herself looking at the boyishly attractive comedian Gordon Andrews. 'Actually, I work on a women's magazine,' she revealed.

His eyes widened humorously. 'How on earth did a member of the press manage to get an invitation here?' He looked around them pointedly at the less-than-well-behaved guests, the champagne flowing liberally, along with the guests' inhibitions.

Andie laughed at his comical expression. 'I'm the senior editor, not a reporter.'

Gordon waggled his dark eyebrows expressively. 'I'd love to see the junior one—she must still be in nappies!'

She liked him, Andie decided, as Gordon seemed to have decided to stay at her side, his wicked brand of humour having her laughing out loud several times through the evening, thankfully diverting her attention away from Adam. Although she was still aware that Adam didn't leave Elizabeth King's side for a single minute, attentively supplying her with champagne and food if she looked like running out of either.

Damn him, Andie decided stubbornly. Stupidly, she had looked forward to this evening out with Adam—and as far as he was concerned she might just as well not exist!

In fact, she was surprised when, the party obviously drawing to a close at about three o'clock in the morning, Adam remembered to come and get her so that the two of them could leave together, she had half expected him to leave with Elizabeth King, too!

'Good party?' Adam finally asked rigidly in the darkness of the car as they drove through the quiet London streets, the rest of the journey having taken place in tension-filled silence.

'Excellent,' Andie came back tautly. 'Gordon Andrews is as funny off stage as he is on it.'

'I noticed you were enjoying yourself,' Adam observed sarcastically.

'Really?' Andie returned just as sarcastically.

Adam turned to her sharply in the confines of the car. 'And exactly what does that mean?' he snapped.

She gave a dismissive shrug of her shoulders. 'Elizabeth King is very beautiful.'

'I—'

'You just missed the turn to my apartment,' she interrupted.

His response was to immediately do an illegal U-turn in the middle of the road—something he wouldn't have stood a chance of doing if it weren't almost four o'clock on a Sunday morning!—bringing the Jaguar to a screeching halt outside the apartment building where she lived, before turning in his seat to look at her with steely grey eyes.

'I would rather have spent the evening with you,' he ground out between clenched jaws.

'Really?' Andie's eyes flashed deeply green in the half-light. 'Then you must have hidden acting ability!' She glared at him, remembering all too clearly that if it hadn't been for Gordon Andrews she would have spent the entire evening mingling with people she didn't know—and who, on this evening's behaviour, she wasn't sure she wanted to know, either!

Adam reached out to grasp her shoulders. 'Are you seeing Andrews again?' he demanded to know—almost as if she had spoken her thoughts out loud!

Andie wrenched out of his grasp, reaching to open her car door—obviously Adam wasn't about to get out and do it for her! 'I don't think that's any of your business!' she scorned as she stepped out onto the pavement.

For such a large man, Adam moved with surprising speed, at her side as she used her key to open the security door at the entrance to the building, following her inside.

He swung her round to face him. 'I'm making it my business, Andie,' he insisted. 'Do you intend seeing Andrews again?' he repeated, his voice steely now.

She looked up at him defiantly. 'I think that's for me to

decide—don't you?' Knowing she actually had no intention of seeing the other man again.

Gordon had asked her if she would like to have dinner with him next week, but, despite having enjoyed his company this evening, Andie knew she wasn't in the least attracted to him. Much better to leave their evening together as a pleasant memory. At least, that part of it!

'Excuse me, Adam,' she dismissed as the lift arrived at the ground floor, stepping inside.

'No,' Adam returned shortly, stepping into the lift beside her. Andie looked at him frowning as the lift ascended to her floor, before stepping out into the carpeted entrance to her apartment, throwing her bag and keys down onto the table and striding through to the calm elegance of her sitting-room.

Adam swung her roughly round to face him, his expression furious in the glow of the side-light she had left on in the room in anticipation of her return.

She gave a heavy sigh, knowing that they were both too angry to continue this conversation. 'It's very late, Adam—'

'That didn't seem to bother you a short time ago when you were all over Gordon Andrews!' he shot back at her, grey eyes glacial.

Her own eyes widened indignantly at his unwarranted accusation. 'The man kept me company for the evening—which is more than can be said of you!' she returned angrily.

'Don't try and turn this round on me,' Adam rasped coldly, his hand tightening on her arm. 'By the time I had concluded my business with Elizabeth you were secluded in a dark corner with that damned clown!'

'I—!' Andie gasped her outrage, trying to pull out of his grasp—and only succeeding in bruising herself instead.

'Elizabeth King is even younger than I am!' she exclaimed. 'Which makes you nothing but a—'

'Yes?' Adam challenged hardly, his face only inches away from her own.

There was a warning in his eyes, but Andie was past caring about his anger, was only concerned with her own humiliation—and hurt, that he should have chosen to spend her coveted evening with him in the company of another woman, a beautifully luring one at that.

She had so looked forward to being with him this evening, had dressed with him in mind—and, as far as she was concerned, he had merely been using her in an effort not to arrive at the party alone, after all!

'An aging Romeo!' Andie concluded stubbornly, anger winning out over prudence.

'An aging—!' Adam's eyes darkened for a moment before they became silvery cold. 'If I'm an aging Romeo,' he bit out tautly, 'then you're nothing but a teasing flirt!'

The two of them glared at each other, nose to nose, green eyes clashing with silver, chins jutting out, neither of them willing to give an inch.

How long they would have gone on staring at each other in that way Andie couldn't have said, but suddenly Adam gave a groan, all of the anger draining out of his body, his hands no longer tight on her arms, the thumbs lightly caressing against the creaminess of her skin.

'Damn you, Andie…!' he breathed raggedly, his forehead damp against hers now.

She felt the change in him, holding her breath in an effort not to break the physical awareness that suddenly seemed to have sprung up between them, her gaze steadily meeting his as she dared him to take this one step further.

'Damn you…!' he groaned again before he moved slightly, his mouth claiming hers.

There was no gentle exploration, no slow rising of passion; as their lips met it was as if a sensual explosion had been set off between them, all thought, all caution, forgotten in the wave of feeling that engulfed them both.

With their mouths still fused in exploration, their clothes fell quickly to the floor, Andie not absolutely sure who took off what, only aware of searing emotion as she felt the naked warmth of Adam's body as it fitted perfectly against her own nakedness, Adam's hands seeking, and finding, each sensitive spot on her body, his lips heatedly following that same trail until Andie felt like liquid fire in his arms.

The carpet felt warm against her back, Adam like fire above her, his lips and hands touching the pouting yearning of her breasts, Andie groaning low in her throat as she felt a nipple drawn completely into the moist heat of Adam's mouth, the gentle touch of his tongue, the pleasure-pain of nibbling teeth, bringing a moist warmth between her thighs.

She arched against him as his hand explored her there, feeling as if she would burst with the heated sensations. And then she did burst, but it was like nothing she had ever known before, every part of her feeling suddenly hypersensitive as the pleasure coursed through her, welcoming Adam into her as his body finally joined with hers.

The pleasure that followed was even more intense than that first time, and as the heated quivering of her body brought Adam to his own peak the two of them reached that unknown plateau together in a sensation that seemed to go on and on into eternity…

His child, he had just said.

Yes, it was Adam's child she carried.

But it was a child that had been conceived in anger rather than love, a fact that had been more than borne out by Adam's dazed expression when he'd raised his head from the dampness of her breasts to look at her with unfocusing, unrecognising grey eyes.

A shiver of shocked reaction quivered through her. Because if Adam hadn't known he was making love with her, then it had to be—Oh, God!

Andie pushed frantically at his chest, feeling a momentary loss as her body ceased to be joined with his, rolling away from him to gather up her shimmering silver gown and hold it protectively in front of her nakedness. 'Go, Adam,' she told him woodenly.

He drew in a short breath, still not quite looking at her. 'I—'

'Just go, Adam,' she bit out, turning away from him so that he shouldn't see the sudden tears that welled up in her pained green eyes. 'Please!'

He swallowed hard, gathering up his own scattered clothes, not speaking again until he was once again fully dressed—and looking remotely unapproachable. 'Andie, I—I don't know what to say,' he began shakily.

Her mouth twisted into the bitter semblance of a smile. 'Then it's probably best that you say nothing,' she told him tersely. Anything he said now could only make the situation worse. If that were possible!

Adam shook his head. 'I don't know what happened,' he said. 'One minute we were furious with each other, the next—!' He gave another shake of his head. 'I'm sorry, Andie,' he added wretchedly.

Not as sorry as she was. Because, in the absence of the woman he really wanted, she had only been a substitute enough like her in looks to allow Adam the fantasy. As Andie knew only too well, that woman was her own, dead, mother!

She knew it as surely as if Adam had spoken the words

out loud—and she knew she would never forgive him for using her in that way.

She stirred herself now, finally opening her eyes to look across the terrace of the villa to where Adam stood grimly in the shadow of the purple bougainvillaea that ran along one side of the mellow stone building.

She knew as she looked at him that, despite everything, she still loved him...!

She hated him.

Adam could see it in the dark green of her eyes as she looked over at him with such cold contempt.

She had never looked lovelier to him, the week she had spent in the warm Majorcan sunshine having given a healthy tan to the silky skin visible above the green bikini, the gentle glow of early pregnancy having given a warm allure to the curves of her body.

That was his child that lay nestled inside that curvaceous body, he acknowledged possessively. His child! And Andie's...

He watched warily as she swung her legs to the floor, sitting up now as she looked across at him with enquiring eyes. It had been this way between them since—since that night, he acknowledged wearily.

He hadn't left her apartment that night only because she'd asked him to. No, he had also seen the shocked dismay in her face when she'd realised what they had just done, a wishing that it had never happened.

He had left her that night knowing they could never go back now, that the easy friendship that had existed between them was no more. That it never would be again.

He hadn't gone straight to his own apartment but had parked his car and walked. And walked. And walked. Desperately trying to find a way back from the dark abyss they had fallen into. There wasn't one, he had finally accepted.

That conclusion had been borne out over the next few weeks, Andie not around whenever he'd visited Rome at the estate. And Andie had returned the flowers he had sent to her office on the Monday morning following that fatal night, having obviously read the card that had accompanied them, her own message written clearly beneath his apology—'Not as sorry as I am!'

Not as sorry as she must have been when she'd found she was pregnant with their child…

Adam moved out of the shadows of the villa, having already removed his jacket on the drive from the airport, the heat of the late August Majorcan sunshine having hit him like a blanket as he'd stepped out of the air-conditioned airport.

'Who told you?' Andie demanded as he came to stand beside her. 'Or do I really need to ask?'

'It wasn't Rome,' Adam assured her softly, looking down at her with hooded eyes, still having difficulty accepting that his child nestled in the warm perfection of her body. It didn't really show yet, only a gentle swell visible to the smoothness of her tummy over the green bikini. 'He is otherwise preoccupied at the moment,' he added derisively.

Andie nodded abruptly, reaching up a hand to the sunglasses that lay amongst her honey-blonde hair, bringing them firmly down over the windows of her eyes. 'I intend returning for the wedding next month,' she revealed.

The two of them had pushed Rome in the right direction where Audrey was concerned and, having proposed and been accepted, Rome was now wasting no time in making Audrey his wife!

Adam's mouth tightened as he thought of the battle he

had in front of him to do the same where Andie was going to fight against accepting that, probably with the last breath of her body!

'So who did tell you, Adam?' Andie prompted.

He wished she didn't have those sunglasses covering the usual candidness of her eyes, wanted to reach out and remove them—but he already knew, from the experience of last weekend, that she would recoil away from him if he tried to touch her. She had done it so many times already...

'I called into your office in the week to see you—'

'Why?' she queried flatly.

Because he hadn't been able to stay away from her any longer! Because he knew she would never voluntarily make a move to see him. Ever again!

'You left last weekend without saying goodbye,' he granted, remembering all too clearly his heart-sinking disappointment the previous Sunday when Audrey had told him Andie had left earlier that morning. Before the two of them had been able to talk any further...

Andie's mouth turned down at the corners. 'I hadn't realised you were such a stickler for good manners, Adam!' she taunted.

He drew in a harsh breath before dropping down onto the lounger next to hers. It hadn't been easy to come here at all, the delays at the airport and subsequent two-hour flight not helping his feelings of trepidation—and his legs were now shaking so badly they wouldn't support him any more!

It hadn't seemed this complicated when he'd been in England. Away from Andie...

He had been shocked to his core when he'd learnt of Andie's pregnancy. But once over that shock, his own part in that pregnancy acknowledged, the way had seemed clear and simple. Andie would have to marry him...

But looking at her now, the unsmiling line of her mouth, the stubborn jut of her chin, Adam knew there was going to be nothing clear or simple about persuading her that a marriage between the two of them was the only answer!

'I'm not,' he answered her taunt, running a hand through the slight dampness of his silver-blond hair. 'I—your assistant editor explained that you're away on—on maternity leave.' And his shock on hearing that hadn't yet receded! 'May I?' he indicated the jug of iced lemonade that sat on the table at her other side, the accompanying glass empty.

'Help yourself,' she invited, standing up before he could reach across her, slipping lightly by him to go and stand at the railing of the terrace, gazing out over the calm blue-green of the Mediterranean Sea.

Adam drank the lemonade thirstily, wishing, as he looked over at the rigid set of Andie's back, that it were whisky. He definitely felt in need of something stronger than lemonade!

'It's beautiful here, isn't it?'' she murmured as he joined her beside the rail.

It was beautiful, the villa built into the terraced hills on the west coast of the island, a one-hundred-and-eighty-degree view of the sea visible as far as the eye could see.

'Peaceful, too,' Andie added with a faint sigh.

It must have been peaceful for her—until he'd arrived, Adam acknowledged heavily. He had been to the villa with Rome and Barbara in the past, its remote spot appealing to the other couple. A woman came in from the village every day with the necessary shopping, staying on to cook and clean, meaning that they didn't have to stir from the villa at all if they didn't want to. As Andie didn't seem to have done...

'I'm sorry, Andie,' Adam said.

Her profile suddenly became rigid as she stared out to

sea, her hands tightly gripping the metal rail. 'I was too, to begin with,' she admitted jerkily. 'But now—somehow I don't seem to mind any more,' she acknowledged softly, her face still averted. But one hand moved protectively to the soft swell of her tummy...

His heart leapt at the admission. Although he knew only too well, from her lack of pleasure in his arrival a few minutes ago, that her feelings towards the baby had nothing to do with him, that maternal instinct was probably the reason for her change of heart.

'I actually meant I was sorry to have interrupted your peace and quiet,' he told her dryly.

Andie glanced at him now, lips twitching as she held back her smile at his humorously raised brows. 'How silly of me.' She shook her head self-derisively.

Adam became serious again. 'I— It seems a little early for maternity leave.' He frowned. 'Is there anything wrong? With you? Or the pregnancy?' His knuckles showed white on the rail as he waited for her answer.

'No,' she assured him lightly. 'I did have a little scare early on—it's okay,' she quickly soothed. 'But Jonas has advised it might be best if I don't continue to work through the pregnancy.'

'So that's how Danie met the man!' he realised. 'She didn't waste any time, did she?' he added ruefully; Andie was only three months pregnant.

Andie laughed. 'Jonas didn't realise what had hit him!'

Adam knew how he felt! The Summer women were absolutely lethal. 'What are we going to do, Andie?' he prompted.

She stiffened defensively, her mouth once again unsmiling. 'I have no idea what you are going to do, Adam,' she said. 'But I am going to soak up the sun for several more weeks, before I have to return for Daddy and Audrey's wedding, and then I will probably stay at the estate until after the baby is born.'

'Not "the" baby—*ours*!' he corrected more harshly than he had meant to.

He couldn't help it; the thought of Andie having their baby still made him shake with reaction. Possessive reaction. He wanted to just gather Andie up, her and the baby, and keep them safe for the rest of their lives.

But one look at Andie's determinedly set features told him it wasn't going to be as easy as that!

'Andie.' He turned to her, gently grasping her shoulders and turning her to face him. Although those damned sunglasses still hid her eyes from him!

'Don't!' she cried, shying away as he would have reached up and removed the sunglasses. 'Why have you come here, Adam? What do you want?'

What did he want? If he told her *that*, she would start running and never look back!

Stay cool, Munroe, he instructed himself severely. Hadn't he already done enough to this woman, without scaring the life out of her with the intensity of his feelings concerning her and their expected baby?

'It's not a question of what I want, Andie,' he ground out. 'It's a question of what is necessary.'

Her chin tilted challengingly. 'And that is...?'

'Marriage!' The word burst out of him forcefully. 'The two of us have to get married, Andie,' he added with grim determination.

She stiffened even more in the grip of his hands, her face first flushing and then becoming translucently pale.

Almost as if he had physically struck her with his suggestion...!

CHAPTER FIVE

MARRIAGE...

How ironic.

How amazingly, incredibly, unbelievably ironic. Marriage was a word Andie had never associated with Adam, and certainly had never matched with her own name.

And it wasn't now. Adam didn't want to marry her, he didn't want to marry anyone. He just felt that he had to...!

'Why are you smiling?' Adam broke harshly into the silence.

Smiling? Was she?

Probably, Andie conceded. What else was there to do in the face of such irony? She loved this man, carried their baby inside her, and he had offered to marry her only because of that baby.

She had known this would happen, of course, had known from the minute he became aware of her pregnancy that Adam would feel compelled to make such an offer.

What alternative did he have? Her father was far from stupid, and, even if neither of them ever revealed to him that it was Adam's baby, their strained manner towards each other, over the months—years?—ahead, would eventually become obvious to Rome. Especially to Rome...! Besides, the baby—son or daughter?—could just look so much like Adam when it was born that there would be no doubt that he was the father.

She looked up at him. 'Poor Adam,' she murmured ruefully.

'Poor—!' His hands tightened on her arms. 'What do you mean by that?' he demanded suspiciously.

She gave a humourless smile. 'A wife would be bad enough, but a child as well! However would you survive, Adam?' she taunted.

'The same way every other father does, I suppose,' he replied. 'With little sleep and a lot of heartache.' He bit out harshly at her questioning look.

That was exactly the way her father had described his own daughters' childhood! Somehow Andie had never thought of Adam in that light...

'You forgot the warmth and laughter,' she told him huskily.

His mouth twitched. 'According to Rome that comes later—once the sleepless nights have stopped! He assures me he walked around in a daze for five years while the three of you were babies!'

Andie gave him a sharp look. 'You haven't talked to my father about—'

'I very much doubt I would be here to tell the tale if Rome knew it was my child!' Adam cut in drily. 'I went to see Rome once I left your office—I needed to know where you had gone—and he assured me he's going to strangle the man if he ever finds out who fathered your baby. Apparently you have been less than helpful on that score...?'

'I have no wish to see you dead—or my father in prison for murdering you!'

Adam's laugh lacked any real humour. 'That could still happen,' he admitted. 'Although I understand your lack of enthusiasm for the latter,' he added grimly.

But not for the former, his words implied. However, despite what he might think to the contrary, she had no wish to see anything happen to Adam. She loved him, for goodness' sake! She just knew it was an emotion he would never reciprocate.

But that didn't mean he couldn't, wouldn't, love their baby. In fact, she was sure that he would. Adam had no family of his own, at least, none that he had ever spoken of, and this baby was his own flesh and blood. His only flesh and blood.

Andie just wasn't sure she could live with him, knowing he loved their child but could never feel anything but affection for her! She wasn't sure—but it was something she had known was going to be offered from the moment when she had decided, a month ago, that she wanted this baby, after all, already loved it with a fierce protectiveness that would allow no harm to come to it. Ever.

But did that include avoiding the emotional trauma that a legal battle with Adam, over his own rights where his child was concerned, would incur...? Did it include standing united with Adam in an effort not to alienate the baby's grandfather from the man who had been his best friend for the last twenty years? Did it include marrying Adam to avoid all that?

She still didn't have the answer to that!

She spoke again, sounding resigned. 'You don't want to marry me, Adam—'

'I don't think what I want—or, indeed, what you want, either!—is of particular importance at this moment,' he shot back, releasing her abruptly to walk determinedly to the other end of the terrace.

Andie swallowed hard, his words having put a chill into her heart. 'It isn't...?'

'No,' he told her firmly, a nerve pulsing in the tightness of his jaw. 'We have to think of the baby—'

'And you think I haven't been?' she cut in angrily, a flush to her cheeks now. 'How dare you?' she accused resentfully. 'Why else would I have given up a job that I love doing, if it weren't because it's safer for the baby if I don't work? Why else would I—?'

'Andie, I wasn't implying—'

'Yes, you were, damn you!' There was something to be said for the emotion of anger. It precluded any others—such as love!—from surfacing. 'And you have no right! You—'

'Andie, I didn't come here to fight with you,' Adam interrupted, eyes glittering silver as he glared across the terrace at her.

'Then why did you come?' Her head went back challengingly.

He gave a heavy sigh. 'I've already told you—I came here to ask you, to plead with you if necessary,' he added hardly, 'to consider marrying me.'

How it pained him to have to say it! What sort of marriage would it be, could it be, when it wasn't what either of them really wanted?

Her chin rose proudly. 'I've considered it, Adam, and—'

'Consider it again!' he advised harshly. 'And this time think of it from another angle but your own!' he continued scathingly, hands clenched at his sides now—as if he might strangle her if he didn't...?

She had been considering *every* angle since the moment she had decided, a month ago, that she loved this baby above everything else; her child's wants and needs were of paramount importance to her now. But she wasn't sure that having parents who didn't love each other was the best thing for her baby...

She gave Adam a narrow-eyed look. 'How can you be absolutely positive this baby is yours, Adam?'

His mouth twisted mockingly. 'I'm sure, Andie.'

'I don't see how—'

'I doubt that experience with me was enough to send you out on a life of bed-hopping conquests,' Adam declared. 'And if it wasn't—! You were a virgin that night, Andie,' he stated flatly. 'Or did you think my life was so debauched I wouldn't recognise a virgin if I met one?'

Andie swallowed hard, turning away, heated colour in her cheeks now. He hadn't said anything at the time—she had thought—

She had spent the last few years of her life living and working amongst a casual permissiveness that simply hadn't appealed to her. Maybe that was because she'd already been in love with Adam, and no other man would do for her; she simply didn't know. But he was right; she had been a virgin that night three months ago…

'You're right.' She sighed defeatedly, not wanting to continue discussing the subject of her virginity—or lack of it now! 'It is your child.'

'I never doubted it,' he bit out forcefully.

'What sort of marriage are you offering me, Adam?' she asked levelly, giving no indication that what he said in the next few minutes could be the deciding point for the rest of their lives.

He looked puzzled. 'I don't understand…?'

'In the circumstances, Adam, surely it's a perfectly straightforward question,' she replied, walking over to sit back down on the lounger. 'Oh, don't worry, I'm not asking for you to pretend you're in love with me. Any more than I could pretend to be in love with you.' How could she pretend something that was already a fact?

His puzzlement deepened. 'Then what are you asking for?' he returned.

Affection—if not love. Respect—surely she deserved that, at least? Fidelity—the one thing she wasn't sure Adam was capable of giving her!

She gave a shaky sigh at the thought of suffering years of women, like Elizabeth King, in the background of Adam's life. She couldn't bear that! But, at the same time, was it really feasible to expect the two of them to live out their lives in a loveless marriage? Oh, not that it would be true of her, but for Adam—!

She took a deep breath. 'The thing is, Adam, I grew up in a large family, and because of that I—I've never believed in having only children.'

He blinked, obviously trying to assimilate her words— and failing. 'You aren't expecting twins, are you?' he gasped.

'Not that I'm aware of, no,' she assured him.

'Then—' He broke off, frowning, his gaze searching on the paleness of her face. 'I see,' he finally said slowly.

'Do you?' She held her breath now as she waited for his answer.

'I think so.' Adam nodded. 'You know, Andie...' he strolled across the terrace to stand beside her '...a lot of what is said, and printed—' he grimaced '—concerning my private life, isn't necessarily all that it appears—'

'If only half of it's true—!' Andie gave a snort of derisive laughter.

'Oh, probably half of it's true,' Adam conceded, sitting down beside her on the lounger, his thigh only inches from the bareness of her own.

Andie was aware of him with every particle of her own body. She had lain naked with this man, made love with him, made a child with him—how could she not be aware of him? She knew she couldn't spend the rest of her life living in close confines with him without—without—

Even so, she flinched as Adam reached out to touch the creamy softness of her cheek, his hand dropping ineffectually down to his side.

He turned to stare grimly across at the tranquil sea. 'It doesn't augur well for those future children you mentioned if you're going to do that every time I try to touch you,' he said bitterly.

Andie paused. He was right, it didn't, but— 'The last time you touched me I got pregnant, remember?' she reminded him.

His mouth quirked. 'Well, that isn't likely to happen again, now, is it?'

She stood up suddenly, moving jerkily away from him. The problem was, just that light touch of Adam's hand on her cheek was enough to make her burn with wanting him, her heart pounding so loudly in her chest she was sure he had to hear it!

Why couldn't she hate this man? It would make life so much simpler. But what had happened between them three months ago precluded her life ever being simple again!

Could she marry Adam, knowing that he didn't love her, but felt forced, because of the baby and his long relationship with all of her family, into offering her marriage?

In retrospect, what had happened between them that night three months ago, seemed so childish, the two of them facing angrily up to each other like a couple of disgruntled children, their lovemaking a result of that immature temper rather than desire.

If she hadn't become pregnant, would they eventually have fallen back into that easy friendship that had been so much a part of their lives for so long?

Somehow she doubted it. But, in reality, it was a question, Andie knew she would never have an answer to...

She drew in a ragged breath, knowing that Adam was still waiting for her answer.

Yes. Or no.

Such simple little words, but one of them would shape the rest of her life. And her baby's...

She was going to say no, he knew it!

Adam had sat watching Andie as the conflicting emotions had flickered across her face: the anger, the sadness, and lastly the resolve. He didn't need a crystal ball to know she was going to turn down his marriage proposal...!

Whatever did he do then?

He would have no choice but to publicly announce the baby was his, not if he wanted to be the baby's father. And he was surprised himself at how much he wanted that. He had never given any thought to having children—you had to be with the woman you loved to think about things like that!—but the mere thought of his child growing inside Andie filled him with pride, and a strange need to be the sort of man the baby deserved as a father.

But if Andie refused to marry him, Adam knew that all hell was going to break loose when he tried to claim his rights as the baby's father. Not that he was bothered about that on his own account; he had struggled through much worse—and lived never to tell the tale, to anyone! No, it was Andie he was worried about. As her husband he could protect her from any, and all, adversity concerning her pregnancy. He didn't think she would allow him to do that if the two of them weren't married. In fact, he would probably become a part of that adversity!

He didn't want ever to hurt Andie—again, that was!—it was just that, circumstances being what they were, he—

'I really have given your suggestion careful consideration, Adam—' the huskiness of her voice interrupted his racing thoughts '—and I've come to the conclusion that—'

'Don't be too hasty, Andie,' he interrupted forcefully. 'As a single mother—even one from an obviously wealthy family,' he added, knowing Rome would never see any of his daughters in financial trouble of any kind, 'there will still be the problems of coping with the child more or less on your own, trying to fit work and motherhood together, of—'

'I've decided to accept your offer, Adam,' Andie put in gently.

'Trying to be everything to the baby and ending up ragged and—' Adam broke off as he realised exactly what Andie had just said.

She was saying yes!

He stared at her, knowing his mouth must literally be hanging open in his shocked surprise. But he couldn't help that; he *was* surprised.

He had expected to have much more of a fight on his hands, knew exactly how independent and strong-willed Andie could be. He had even booked a one-way ticket over here because he hadn't been sure how long it would take him to persuade Andie that marriage to him was by far the best solution. For all of them...

Instead she had said yes to his marriage proposal, not exactly instantly, but not with too much delay either.

He looked across at her with narrowed eyes, suspicion in their silver depths. 'What's the catch?' he murmured slowly, sure there had to be one. Although for the life of him he couldn't think what it could be!

Andie laughed softly, shaking her head, her hair a honey-coloured tumble over the bareness of her shoulders. 'I'm sure that isn't the normal reply when a woman has just accepted your marriage proposal!'

Adam remained unsmiling. 'This isn't a normal marriage proposal,' he pointed out gruffly.

'No,' she sobered, turning away. 'However, I do accept,

Adam,' she told him flatly. 'And there is no catch,' she added. 'Except—'

'Aha,' he pounced. '"Except" is definitely a catch.' He was frowning darkly now. 'What are your conditions for accepting, Andie?' he asked warily.

If she gave their marriage a time period, he couldn't accept; it was either for ever or not at all. If she asked for a marriage of convenience, again he couldn't accept; that one time with Andie had shown him that he couldn't promise never to make love to her again.

He wanted her now, couldn't even look at her without feeling aroused by her beauty and the smooth perfection of her body. Not that he did intend making love to her again until they were married, he just knew there was absolutely no way he could agree to a platonic marriage—because he would break that promise the minute she was his wife!

She stilled awhile before turning to look at him. At least, Adam presumed she was looking at him; those wretched sunglasses made it impossible to see exactly where she was looking!

'Take off the sunglasses, Andie,' he instructed harshly before she could speak. 'I want to see your eyes, damn it,' he ground out at her surprised expression.

'The windows to the soul, hmm, Adam?' she responded. But she reached up anyway and pushed the dark glasses back up into her hair.

'Something like that,' he said distractedly, looking searchingly into those deep green depths. And learnt nothing. Andie was deliberately keeping all expression out of her face and eyes... 'You were saying...?' he prompted gently, finding himself tensed as if waiting for a blow.

Perhaps he was. If Andie's conditions included either of those two things he knew he simply couldn't accept, then they were going to be in trouble

She gave him a wry look. 'Now it's your turn to give this serious thought, Adam,' she taunted. 'We obviously aren't marrying for the reason people usually decide to spend the rest of their lives together. So far, it would appear that neither of us has met that one person we simply can't live without—'

'If you're talking about falling in love, Andie, then say so!' he interrupted, not liking the way this conversation was going at all.

She gave a taut smile, shrugging slightly. 'Okay, I'm talking about falling in love,' she confirmed with sarcasm. 'And until such time as either of us actually does that, I would want our marriage to be on a one-to-one basis—'

'Hell, I'm sure you never used to be this evasive!' Adam exploded as he stood up. 'What you're really trying to say is that if we get married you would expect me to be faithful—'

'*Both* of us to be faithful,' she corrected, her expression strained now.

'Until such time as either one of us meets that one person we can't live without,' Adam scathingly echoed her earlier words, shaking his head as he came to stand beside her, hands clenched tensely at his sides. 'I'm sorry, but your condition isn't acceptable to me, Andie,' he stated.

She paled, her cheeks suddenly looking translucent, giving her a fragile appearance that Adam instantly found alarming. But he couldn't agree to her condition; it would be like living with a sword hanging over his head. He had decided long ago, if marriage was ever for him, then it would have to be for ever. He couldn't—wouldn't—accept less. There was simply no way he could spend the rest of his life living in fear that Andie, of all people, might one day fall in love with someone else, and consequently leave him! No way…!

'Try to see it from my point of view, Andie,' he cajoled, still alarmed by her paleness. 'You're being unreasonable—'

'I should have known I was asking too much,' she cut in, giving him a disgusted glance before dropping those concealing sunglasses back down on the bridge of her nose. 'You're offering only half a commitment, Adam, for the sake of our child. I'm sorry, but I couldn't live that way.' She turned away, her face set in rigid lines.

Adam grasped her arms, turning her back to face him. 'You couldn't live that way?' he echoed disbelievingly. 'Then why the hell should you expect me to?' He shook her slightly in his agitation. 'From what I understand, marriage can be difficult enough, without having to sit there waiting for your partner to fall in love with someone else!'

Andie opened her mouth to say something. And then closed it again, looking up at him frowningly.

Adam coldly withstood that searching gaze. He would do a lot for Andie, agree to almost anything she asked of him, but he could not agree to committing himself to sitting there wondering when she would leave him. He just couldn't do that.

She hesitated. 'I didn't—I wasn't—Adam, I think there's been some sort of misunderstanding—'

'No misunderstanding, Andie,' he bit back. 'Either you agree to marry me, on the understanding it's a lifetime commitment—with no third parties involved. Ever,' he added grimly. 'Or we forget the whole thing.'

His heart was beating so loudly in his chest he could almost hear it, the blood rushing through his veins at breakneck speed as he felt his future balanced on the knife-edge of Andie's reply. He hadn't meant to issue her with an ultimatum, but in the circumstances he didn't feel he had any option. Even so, he stopped breathing as he waited for her to speak.

A nerve pulsed erratically in the slender column of Andie's throat. 'Adam,' she began slowly. 'Just now, when you said those terms were unacceptable to you, I thought you meant that fidelity to me was unacceptable to you, not—' she licked the dryness of her lips '—not the—the fact that the marriage might eventually fail because one of us fell in love with someone else!'

Adam's lips thinned. 'I may have come into the idea of marriage a bit later than most people, Andie, but that doesn't mean I don't have my own views on what it should be. And it shouldn't be a relationship that has the sword of Damocles hanging over it!'

That nerve was still pulsing in her throat, but some of the colour seemed to be returning to her cheeks now. Thank goodness, Adam noted with relief. He had come here to offer a solution to their problem, not to make Andie ill.

Her body relaxed slightly beneath the tight hold Adam still had of her arms. 'I agree,' she finally said softly.

Adam was perturbed. What did she agree to? This was turning into a nightmare; his emotions were like a roller coaster, one minute up, the next minute down.

Andie drew in a steadying gulp of air, her chin raised determinedly. 'On the understanding that it won't be a temporary thing. No half commitments, no third parties involved. Ever,' she repeated his words clearly. 'I agree to marry you.'

That knife-edge was suddenly no longer there, the sword no longer threatening. Andie was going to marry him!

And for the moment, that would have to be enough...

CHAPTER SIX

THE angry bellow could be heard throughout the whole house. Although the house staff, thank goodness, were used, over the years, not to react to their employer's occasional bouts of temper, apparently carrying on with their daily chores.

Something Andie was most grateful for as she shot Audrey a pained grimace. The two of them were in the sitting-room, supposedly drinking coffee together. Although, so far, that coffee had remained cooling in the cups as the two of them sat tensely waiting for Rome's reaction to Adam's news.

They had just heard it!

'It's gone very quiet,' Andie murmured a few seconds later, straining her ears trying to hear any further reaction from her father. The house remained silent with expectation. Unlike Andie, who was expecting, but certainly couldn't remain silent. Especially if her father were now in the process of doing Adam some physical damage. After all, she had been there three months ago too...! 'Do you think I should—?'

'No, I don't,' Audrey answered calmly, finally reaching forward to pick up her coffee-cup and sip at the now tepid liquid.

'But Rome might—'

'He won't,' Audrey assured her with certainty, looking serenely beautiful as she sat in one of the armchairs.

Andie wished she had the older woman's control! But she didn't, standing up to pace agitatedly up and down the room, glancing towards the doorway often, the two men ensconced in Rome's study down the carpeted hallway.

'How can you be so sure?' Andie finally burst out, the lack of any noise whatsoever coming from the direction of the study grating on her already frayed nerves. 'I realise that your engagement, and the wedding next month, have calmed Daddy down a lot, but even so, he isn't going to be pleased by what Adam's telling him, is he?' A frown marred her creamy brow.

'You might be surprised,' Audrey came back dryly. 'Oh, not by his reaction to your and Adam's news,' she added at Andie's obvious surprise at the remark. 'His reaction to that is anyone's guess, I'm afraid. No, I was referring to Rome's calmness.' She shook her head. 'He isn't calm at all since I told him that I had lived here, and worked for him, for twelve years, without going to bed with him, and that now I intended to wait until our wedding night!'

Andie gave a choked laugh, her own worries temporarily forgotten. 'You told Rome that?'

'I certainly did.' The older woman returned her smile. 'My assurance that anticipation is half the fun didn't go down too well, either!' she confided mischievously.

'I'm sure it didn't.' Andie laughed out loud now, easily able to imagine her father's frustration with such a decision. Although he still looked a lot happier than Andie had seen him for years. At least, he *had* looked happier... Her smile faded, to be replaced by her previous frown. 'But you must have some idea of what Rome's going to say about—about—' She still had trouble formulating the words herself. 'I wanted to tell Daddy myself, but Adam insisted he had to be the one to do it,' she went on, irritated beyond words at what she considered Adam's chauvinist behaviour.

In fact, what she had really wanted to happen was for Adam to return to England after their talk, while she stayed on in Majorca for another week. But Adam wouldn't hear of it. They either both stayed in Majorca, or they both returned to England. And he had been absolutely adamant that he would be the one to talk to Rome.

'Quite right too.' Audrey nodded. 'It's his responsibility, Andie,' she added firmly before Andie could protest.

'Don't be ridiculous, Audrey. I'm almost twenty-six years old; I knew exactly what I was doing when I made love with Adam.'

Just once, she had promised herself at a point in their lovemaking when she had known she could have stopped it if she had wanted to. Just once, to be held in Adam's arms, to be loved for herself, and not for her resemblance to her mother. Just once—and it was turning into a lifetime commitment for both of them!

It was going to be no easy thing to be Adam's wife, to know that she could only ever be second best. But any woman would have been second best after her mother, so why not let it be her? After all, she loved Adam, and maybe one day—one day, he might be able to love her a little in return. Better, Andie had decided in Majorca, to be with the man she loved, than spend the rest of her life doing what she had already done for so long: watching and loving him from afar...

Audrey gave her a searching look. 'I'm sure you did,' she finally said. 'As did Adam. Which is why he should be the one to tell your father.' She gave a smile. 'Rome is so overjoyed at the idea of being a grandfather, he might just decide to overlook the fact that the two of you didn't get married first. I—' She broke off as a door could be heard opening down the hallway. 'I think we're about to find out,' Audrey revised quickly.

Andie could feel her tension growing as the two men made their slow progress down the hallway. At least, it seemed slow to her, they could actually have been running for all she knew!

Her father was the first to enter the sitting-room, a quick search of his rigidly set features telling her nothing, her gaze quickly passing to Adam, her heart sinking as he gave a slight shake of his head.

Whatever did that mean? Even if her father wasn't agreeable to them getting married, they were adults, for goodness' sake, could do as they pleased. They had done exactly that three months ago, which was why they were here together today at all! They had only come here to tell her father of their plans; they weren't asking his permission!

Having agonised as she had over accepting Adam's marriage proposal in the first place, she certainly wasn't about to let her father put a dampener on it now!

'I won't have it, Andie,' her father's angrily grated comment broke the tense silence. 'It's just not on. No daughter of mine—'

'Daddy, this has nothing to do with you,' she broke in determinedly; having made her decision where marrying Adam was concerned—painfully so!—she wasn't about to have her father now telling her what she could and couldn't do! 'I'm over eighteen, have been making my own decisions for years now, and Adam and I have only come here today to pay you the courtesy of letting you know what our plans are. You—'

'Very kind of you, I'm sure!' Rome exclaimed sarcastically.

'Andie—'

'Leave it, Adam,' the older man told him sharply as he would have interrupted. 'I don't believe my daughter has finished speaking yet.' Rome turned pointedly back to Andie. 'You were saying…?'

She drew in a ragged breath. 'Adam and I—' She

stopped, wondering if she would ever get used to hearing their two names linked together like that. 'We have decided to get married. We would naturally like you and Audrey to be there, but—'

'How kind of you again,' her father drawled, lowering his lean length into one of the armchairs, chilly blue gaze fixed on Andie.

She shifted uncomfortably under the intensity of that gaze. 'We intend getting a special licence, and the wedding will be organised in a register office for the end of next week—'

'No,' her father stated decisively.

Andie's cheeks flushed mutinously. 'It isn't your decision, Daddy,' she burst out incredulously, looking across at Adam appealingly. Instead of just standing there, why didn't he do something, say something? 'I am going to marry Adam, Rome,' she began again. 'With or without your approval. Although, of course, I would rather have it—'

'Again, how kind,' Rome said dryly.

Her cheeks flushed fiery red at his obvious continued sarcasm.

'But I don't need it,' she told him determinedly. 'And your permission I certainly don't need.'

'Andie.' Adam spoke quietly as he crossed the room to her side, his arm moving protectively about her shoulders. 'Rome, stop playing with her,' he turned to tell the older man. 'Andie, your father is perfectly in agreement with the two of us getting married,' he told her gently.

'How kind of *you*!' she snapped rebelliously at her father.

'He just isn't happy,' Adam continued, 'with the two of us going to a register office to do it!'

'My exact words were, sneaking off to a register office

to do it,' Rome said. 'Harrie and Danie have had full white weddings,' he continued. 'You and Adam will have the same.'

Andie stared at her father. He—they—what—? 'You don't disapprove of my marrying Adam...!' she realised dazedly.

'Certainly not,' Rome came back instantly. 'I'm actually amazed you've shown such good taste.'

'Thanks!' She was still dazed at his reaction.

'I'm not too pleased by the way the two of you have been creeping about meeting each other in secret,' Rome commented. 'But other than that, I couldn't have chosen a better husband for you myself!' he added with satisfaction.

Andie had turned to give Adam a sharp look at her father's mention of the two of them meeting each other in secret, the tightening of Adam's arm about her shoulders, and his warning glance, telling her he would explain later. When the two of them were alone...

Not that he needed to explain; she could already guess how the conversation had gone between Adam and her father. Adam could hardly have told the older man that the two of them had actually only been out together once, and that Rome's grandchild was the result of anger with each other over the way that evening had turned out!

She just wished Adam had taken the trouble to explain to her exactly how he was going to broach the subject to her father! Although, in truth, the two of them had barely spoken to each other on the flight back to England earlier in the day.

She turned back to her father. 'We can't get married in church, Daddy,' she told him huskily. 'I— It wouldn't seem right. In the circumstances I certainly can't get married in white!' She was slightly pale now, the strain of this meeting finally getting to her.

'Sit down,' Adam told her firmly, pushing her gently down into a chair before pouring some fresh coffee into her cup and handing it to her. 'Drink it,' he instructed evenly, standing over her.

After a rebellious moment of stubbornness, Andie did exactly that, her eyes flashing deeply green as she glared at her future husband over the rim of the cup.

Rome chuckled gleefully. 'Out of the frying pan, hmm, Andie?' he teased with obvious enjoyment of the situation.

She shook back her hair as she turned to include her father in that glare. Adam was as forceful as her father, all right. And as domineering. Which meant the two of them were probably going to have more than their fair share of arguments before they came to some sort of compromise. But that would probably be preferable to the two of them continuing to behave like polite strangers!

'Andie, you don't have to wear white for the wedding.' Audrey was the one to step tactfully into the rising tension. 'Most women wear cream nowadays, anyway. Or almond, even. It's a sad reflection on society, I know, but I'm afraid there aren't too many virgin brides left any more!'

Andie deliberately didn't look at Adam as her cheeks coloured fiery red, but she could sense his searching glance on her. Except for that one act of heated impetuosity between the two of them, they both knew she *would* have been a virgin bride.

'Don't you think I'll look slightly ridiculous?' Andie began sharply. 'Floating down the aisle on the arm of my father, over three months pregnant!'

'No.' Adam was the one to answer. 'You'll just look beautiful. As you always do,' he added emotionally.

This was going to be a nightmare, Andie decided. They had overcome the hurdle of her father's anger and disapproval, only to find themselves confronted with the prospect of a church wedding rather than the register office Andie would have preferred— That *she* would have preferred...?

She turned sharply to look at Adam, his deadpan expression telling her nothing of his thoughts. Deliberately so? He hadn't said anything in Majorca when she had told him she wanted a quiet wedding, as unobtrusive as possible, with only close family in attendance. At the time she had assumed his silence on the subject had been agreement, now she wasn't so sure...

'It just seemed better to tell your father we had been meeting in secret,' Adam defended wearily at her attack. 'After thinking about it—'

'For all of two seconds,' Andie accused, the two of them sitting in Adam's car as he drove them back to London.

Adam accepted it had been an evening of tension for the two of them, the subject of the wedding—in church—the only conversation over dinner.

'What would you rather I had done, Andie?' Adam challenged, hands tightly gripping the steering wheel. 'Explain to Rome that we only went out together for the evening once—and his grandchild is the result of that evening?'

Of course Andie wouldn't want that. And Adam had known that only too well. But Adam could also understand Andie's problem with that; this way Rome, and the rest of her family, were going to assume this was a love-match...

'Of course not.' She sighed wearily. 'But how do you expect the two of us to keep up this obligation we now feel to act as if we're in love with each other?'

His mouth set grimly. 'We would have had to do that anyway, Andie, you know that,' he said. 'Rome wouldn't accept anything less for one of his daughters.'

If Rome so much as guessed this situation was at all contrived, then he wouldn't have given his blessing to their marriage. Despite what Andie might have claimed earlier, Adam knew her well enough to know she would find any estrangement from her father extremely stressful. And, in her condition, that simply wasn't on as far as Adam was concerned.

'It wasn't so bad this evening, was it?' he asked teasingly, sensing rather than seeing the sharp look she gave him in the dark confines of the car. 'I thought we managed quite well,' he opined with satisfaction.

'And I think you went too damned far when you tried to tempt me into eating dessert by actually feeding it to me yourself!' Andie replied impatiently.

That was a pity; he had quite enjoyed that part of the evening! 'But you enjoyed the dessert, after all, didn't you?' he reasoned sardonically, having eventually persuaded her to eat every mouthful of the sherry trifle.

'It isn't a question of enjoying it,' Andie said snappily. 'I simply don't want to end up as big as a house before the baby is born!'

Adam looked at her darkly at his explanation. 'I think your size ten can go to hell for the time being!'

'Size eight, actually,' she came back waspishly. 'And I have no intention of battling for months to regain my figure after the baby is born.'

Adam opened his mouth to tell her once again exactly what he thought about the subject of her weight, and then closed it again. He didn't want to argue with Andie, especially over something he knew, in the long run, he would have very little say in. Andie would do as she pleased. He had enough confidence in her judgement to know she would never do anything that would harm the baby.

'Are we having our first engaged argument?' He finally broke the silence.

'We aren't engaged, Adam,' she came back tautly.

'Oh, yes, we are,' he returned as determinedly. 'We agreed in Majorca that we're both only going to do this the once, Andie, so we're going to do it properly. I've asked you to marry me, you've accepted—'

'You asked because I'm pregnant. And I accepted—'

'For the same reason,' he pointed out. 'But I suggest we both move on from there. I—'

'Adam, was it your idea we get married in church?' she prompted suspiciously.

He drew in a sharp breath. 'Rome—'

'No, not Rome,' she insisted, turning in her seat to look at him. 'Oh, I'm sure he was in full agreement with it, but who was the first one to suggest it?'

She was too damned astute by half, Adam decided frustratedly. 'I was,' he admitted reluctantly.

'I thought so!' Andie exclaimed irritably.

His mouth firmed. 'And can you honestly say you wouldn't prefer a church wedding?'

She sighed. 'In all honesty, no. But—'

'No buts, Andie,' he said with finality. 'A church wedding it will be. Tomorrow we will meet, choose an engagement ring together, before going out for a celebration lunch.'

'No!' Andie gasped protestingly.

'You would rather we had lunch and then chose the engagement ring?' he reasoned thoughtfully. 'I don't see how we can celebrate when we don't have the ring yet, but—'

'No, that isn't what I meant at all, and you know it,' she interjected with reluctant laughter. 'Adam—'

'Yes, Andrea?' he returned mildly.

'Uh-oh,' she said warily. 'Rome only ever calls me by my full name when I've pushed him as far as he's willing to go...'

Adam knew that. 'Yes?' he prompted again.

'Okay, okay.' She held up her hands defensively. 'An engagement ring and then lunch it is.'

Adam reached out and squeezed her hand. 'I knew you would come round to my way of thinking.'

'I'm not sure I had any say in it at all,' she replied. 'I hope you aren't going to be this domineering over everything, Adam. Because if you are—'

'We're going to end up arguing a lot,' he predicted lightly. 'And that isn't going to be good for you or—'

'The baby,' Andie put in dryly.

'Or me,' Adam finished correctly. 'I've never liked arguments, Andie.' Probably because he had witnessed too many of them in his formative years, and the thought of living in that sort of battlefield gave him the shudders! 'Any problems, and I suggest we talk them out rather than resort to a slanging match, okay?'

'I've never resorted to a slanging match in my life—'

'Good,' he cut in with satisfaction over Andie's outraged outburst. 'That's agreed, then.'

The indignant silence emanating from Andie's side of the car told him she didn't think she had agreed to anything!

Adam inwardly acknowledged this new relationship with Andie was slightly odd. Although not in an unpleasant way. No, he decided happily, not unpleasant at all...

In fact, he knew he could get used to it all too quickly!

'Shall I come in with you?' Adam offered once he had parked the car outside her apartment building, getting out to open her door for her.

Andie joined him on the pavement. 'What on earth for?' she asked.

'Now there's a leading question...' he teased.

'Don't be ridiculous, Adam.' Her cheeks were fiery red as she looked up at him.

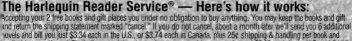

The Harlequin Reader Service® — Here's how it works:

Accepting your 2 free books and gift places you under no obligation to buy anything. You may keep the books and gift and return the shipping statement marked "cancel." If you do not cancel, about a month later we'll send you 6 additional novels and bill you just $3.34 each in the U.S., or $3.74 each in Canada, plus 25¢ shipping & handling per book and applicable taxes if any.* That's the complete price and — compared to cover prices of $3.99 each in the U.S. and $4.50 each in Canada — it's quite a bargain! You may cancel at any time, but if you choose to continue, every month we'll send you 6 more books, which you may either purchase at the discount price or return to us and cancel your subscription.

*Terms and prices subject to change without notice. Sales tax applicable in N.Y. Canadian residents will be charged applicable provincial taxes and GST.

If offer card is missing write to: Harlequin Reader Service, 3010 Walden Ave., P.O. Box 1867, Buffalo NY 14240-1867

NO POSTAGE
NECESSARY
IF MAILED
IN THE
UNITED STATES

BUSINESS REPLY MAIL
FIRST-CLASS MAIL   PERMIT NO. 717-003   BUFFALO, NY

POSTAGE WILL BE PAID BY ADDRESSEE

HARLEQUIN READER SERVICE
3010 WALDEN AVE
PO BOX 1867
BUFFALO NY 14240-9952

Play The *Lucky Hearts* Game

and get...

FREE BOOKS & a FREE GIFT...
YOURS to KEEP!

Yes! I have scratched off the silver card. Please send me my **2 FREE BOOKS** and **FREE MYSTERY GIFT**. I understand that I am under no obligation to purchase any books as explained on the back of this card.

Scratch Here!
then look below to see
what your cards get you...

306 HDL DC5R   **106 HDL DC5H**

| | | | | | | | | | | | | | | | | | |

NAME   (PLEASE PRINT CLEARLY)

ADDRESS

APT.#   CITY

STATE/PROV.   ZIP/POSTAL CODE

Twenty-one gets you
2 FREE BOOKS and a
FREE MYSTERY GIFT!

Twenty gets you
2 FREE BOOKS!

Nineteen gets you
1 FREE BOOK!

TRY AGAIN!

Visit us online at
www.eHarlequin.com

'You're probably right,' he agreed. 'Exactly when are Danie and Jonas expected back from their honeymoon?'

'This weekend,' Andie provided with a puzzled frown. 'Why?'

'We'll make an appointment to go and see Jonas on Monday.'

'Monday?' Andie echoed incredulously. 'I'll have you know that Jonas is a very busy man. I very much doubt he will have the time to see us on Monday.'

Adam quirked blonde brows. 'He couldn't make time even for his new sister-in-law and her fiancé?'

Her cheeks flushed fiery red. 'I have never asked for special favours in any part of my life!'

No, he was aware of that. Andie had worked her way up to her now prominent position as Senior Editor of *Gloss*, even though her father had been more than capable of buying her the magazine if she had ever expressed such a wish. Which she never had. But Andie's independence was part of what he admired about her.

'I'll call Jonas's office anyway,' he said purposefully.

'But why do you need to see him?' Andie frowned her consternation. 'I've already told you that the pregnancy is progressing well after that hiccup a few weeks ago.'

Adam's mouth tightened. 'I want to hear more about that "hiccup", and its implications.'

'But—'

'You'll just have to accept, Andie, that I intend being one-hundred-per-cent involved in your pregnancy, and the birth,' he told her. 'Besides, I need to have a chat with Jonas, anyway.'

'Concerning what?' Andie eyed him suspiciously.

'Concerning how and when it's going to be safe for us to indulge in anything like that,' Adam answered mildly.

'Indulge in anything like what?' Andie cried.

'Like that,' he repeated, suppressing the laughter he felt at Andie's obvious indignation, not sure she would appreciate his humour in her present mood. In fact, he was sure she wouldn't.

But he had realised from her flinching reaction to him in Majorca that they had a few barriers to break down on the side of any physical relationship they intended having in the future. And, as husband and wife, they *would* have a physical relationship.

They were two healthy, not unattractive people, about to marry each other; there was no way they could live celibate together. Besides, Andie had told him quite clearly that she wanted more than one child...

Andie stiffened her shoulders, green eyes flashing fire as she glared at him. 'In my opinion, anything like that can wait until after we're married!' she growled.

He shrugged. 'I'm sure Jonas would allow a few kisses and caresses—'

'Maybe Jonas would—but I wouldn't!' Andie told him furiously.

'We don't want to get out of practice,' he drawled mockingly.

Her fingers tightened on the strap of her handbag. 'Some of us have never been *in* practice,' she responded scathingly. 'And a week or so's abstinence won't do you any harm, either!'

A week or so...

How little she knew. Adam hadn't so much as looked at another woman since that night with Andie almost four months ago.

As he looked at the flushed beauty of her face, inwardly indulging himself with the knowledge that she carried their baby, he had a feeling that he never would again...

CHAPTER SEVEN

She was being stupid. Ridiculous. Juvenile.

But somehow, no matter what names she called herself, Andie couldn't help her feelings of excitement as she waited for Adam to arrive to take her out to choose their engagement ring.

He had kissed her very chastely on the cheek last night before leaving her with the promise that he would pick her up at eleven o'clock today.

Andie had dressed with care, the Edwardian-style jacket of the bottle-green suit she wore doing much to hide the slighter fullness to her waist and breasts, the cream blouse alleviating its dark colour. Her hair was thick and glossily gold over her shoulders, her make-up light, peach lipgloss emphasising the curve of her mouth.

Power-dressing, her father would have called it. But, as Andie was quickly learning, she needed all the confidence she could muster against Adam's teasing forcefulness.

She had wanted to be the one to talk to her father, but Adam had insisted it had to be him that did that. She hadn't expected a church wedding, but Adam had seen to it that was exactly what they would have. She hadn't expected an engagement ring, either. But again, she had been overruled.

She would have to be very careful in the future that Adam didn't end up making all their decisions for them!

But when she opened the door to him a few minutes later, eyes widening as she took in his handsomeness in the charcoal-grey suit and pale silver shirt, a grey silk tie knotted neatly at his throat, Andie realised it wasn't going to

99

be so easy to withstand his way of charming her into agreement. Not if her knees knocked together like this every time she saw him!

Adam bent his head to lightly brush his lips against hers. 'You look beautiful,' he told her as he straightened. 'I've booked an appointment for us at the jewellers for eleven-thirty, with instructions for them to show us rings that have emeralds in as well as diamonds. And the restaurant is booked for—'

'I can see you've been very busy this morning, Adam,' Andie interrupted. 'But shouldn't you have consulted me first about the type of engagement ring I would like? You—'

'I thought the emeralds would go with your eyes.' He shrugged. 'But if you have other ideas...?'

An emerald and diamond engagement ring sounded wonderful, especially in view of the fact that until yesterday she hadn't known she was going to have one at all. But, even so, Adam instructing the jewellers that was what they were to show her was just another example of his high-handedness.

'Not particularly,' she dismissed, turning to pick up her bag. 'I would just like to do my own choosing, if you don't mind.'

'I don't mind at all,' he accepted, taking a light hold of her arm as they left the apartment. 'Your father has some good news too. He's managed to secure a church wedding for us at three o'clock three weeks on Saturday,' he announced.

'It's not what you know but who you know,' Andie muttered, her earlier excitement giving way to irritation. She had the feeling much like being on a runaway express train—with her merely a helpless passenger!

'Quite honestly, Andie, I don't care how Rome managed

it,' Adam stated as he held the car door open for her to get inside. 'Besides, that extra couple of weeks will allow time for any other arrangements we want to make.'

'It will also allow time for me to look even more pregnant,' Andie pointed out.

Adam turned to smile at her as he got into the car beside her. 'I told you, Andie; you look beautiful. Pregnancy obviously suits you.'

She was also, she inwardly acknowledged, starting to sound like a shrill-voiced harridan. She really didn't have any objection to any of these arrangements—apart from the fact that her father and Adam seemed to have taken over! Besides, she didn't want Adam to think he was getting a shrew for a wife...

'I'm sure it will all work out,' she replied noncommittally.

Adam reached out and squeezed her hand. 'I'm going to be the model husband and father,' he assured her huskily.

Andie couldn't help it, she spluttered with laughter. 'Now that I just have to see,' she chuckled once she felt able to talk again. 'Adam Munroe, one of the world's most eligible bachelors, a model husband and father! Do you have any idea how to go about achieving that?'

Adam arched arrogant brows at her laughter. 'Your father managed it, so why shouldn't I?'

Her humour faded completely. Her father had 'managed' it because Barbara had been his wife and the mother of his children; Adam only had her.

'Perhaps you're right,' she responded flatly, turning to look sightlessly out of the car window.

She had known in Majorca, when she'd accepted Adam's proposal, that this marriage was going to be fraught with emotional tension. But actually living it was completely different from knowing it...

'What did I say wrong now?' Adam asked softly at her continued silence.

Andie forced her panicked feelings back into the recesses of her mind. There was no reason, absolutely none, she told herself firmly, why her marriage to Adam shouldn't be a complete success.

'Nothing.' She reached out and lightly touched his arm.

The choosing of her engagement ring was much more fun than she had imagined it would be, Adam's indulgence knowing no bounds as he encouraged her to try on any ring that took her fancy.

There were no prices on any of the rings—the exclusivity of the jewellers clearly indicated that if you needed to know the price then you couldn't afford it!—but even so some of the jewels were so big as to be garish in Andie's eyes.

The ring she finally settled on was definitely not in that category, an emerald and diamond cluster, one large emerald surrounded by eight smaller diamonds.

'There is a wedding ring to complement this particular ring,' the male assistant told them.

'I—'

'We'll look at it,' Adam answered the man firmly. 'And a plain gold wedding ring is suitable for me,' he added decisively.

Andie turned slowly to look at him as the male assistant moved unhurriedly to get the requested rings. Adam intended wearing a wedding ring?

He looked at her in amusement at her obvious surprise. 'A model husband and father, remember?' he teased.

'And that includes wearing a wedding ring?' She couldn't say she wasn't pleased that Adam intended to wear this public announcement of being a married man; she was just stunned that he was choosing to do so.

'Yes, it does,' he told her with certainty. 'I—'

'Here we are, sir, madam.' The assistant returned with the matching wedding ring to Andie's choice of engagement ring, and another tray containing an assortment of male wedding rings.

Her own wedding ring was shaped to fit around the cluster, also studded with emeralds and diamonds. But, to Andie's amazement, Adam took as much time choosing his wedding ring as she had her engagement ring, finally settling on a thin plain gold band. She had to admit, it suited the long, artistic slenderness of his hand.

Although Adam wasn't quite so happy with his own choice when Andie insisted on buying it for him!

'That was unnecessary,' he told her stiltedly when they left the shop a short time later, Andie's engagement ring firmly on her finger, the two wedding rings packed away in their respective boxes.

Andie reached out and touched his arm. 'Not to me,' she assured him. If he intended wearing a wedding ring, then it was going to be one that she had bought for him. Otherwise it just wouldn't mean the same thing.

He seemed about to say something else, but then thought better of it. 'Thank you,' he finally accepted.

She gave a mischievous smile. 'You're welcome. Not very good at accepting gifts yourself, are you?' Her own rings must have cost several hundred times more than Adam's wedding ring had cost her.

He grimaced. 'Probably because I've very rarely been given any.'

Andie looked up at him thoughtfully. 'Not even when you were a child?' she probed gently, realising, and not for the first time, just how little she really knew about his early years.

Adam gave a bitter laugh. 'Especially not then!'

'But—'

'Leave it, Andie,' he grated. 'I promise I'll try to be a little more gracious about accepting the next time you give me a gift, okay?' he added with deliberate lightness.

But Andie wasn't fooled for a moment. What sort of parents had he had not to know the joy of receiving gifts from them at Christmas and on his birthday…?

There was still so much about Adam she didn't know, so many facets she wasn't aware of that had made him the man he was today. Well, maybe she didn't know them now. But she would. Oh, yes, in time she most definitely would!

Adam watched her face as they entered the dining-room of the restaurant he had booked for lunch, knowing by the pleasure that lit up her features as she saw her father and Audrey already seated there, along with Andie's sister Harrie and her husband Quinn, that he had done the right thing in inviting them here to share in their celebration.

Up until this moment, he could only hope that he was doing the right thing in organising this surprise for her. Although he had also realised that by presenting a *fait accompli* to her family today it was going to be less awkward for Andie in the future; the last thing she wanted, or needed, at the moment was to go around explaining herself to all of them.

'We'll go out with Danie and Jonas separately once they're back from their honeymoon,' he assured Andie as they went to join the rest of her family at the table.

She turned to give him a glowing smile, emerald-coloured eyes over-bright with unshed tears. 'Thank you.' She squeezed his arm gratefully.

They might have started this off all wrongly, Adam had decided as he'd lain alone in his bed the previous evening, but that stopped right here. Andie deserved to have the best, and a celebration lunch for their engagement was going to be the start of it.

'My, my, my,' Harrie said as she stood up to congratulate them both. 'Some people will go to any lengths to throw a party!'

Andie laughed softly. 'It's Adam's party.'

'Our party,' he corrected firmly.

Harrie reached up to kiss him warmly on the cheek. 'You've been an honorary member of our family for so long, it will be nice to make it official.' She smiled at him.

Adam glanced at Andie, realising she was very close to letting those tears overflow and spill hotly down her cheeks. 'Show Harrie and Audrey your ring, Andie,' he instructed teasingly. 'While us men get down to the more serious matter of studying the menus!'

Lunch was a resounding success, Andie relaxing completely in the company of her family, laughingly happy, even indulging in a sip of the champagne Adam ordered for a celebration toast.

Now all he had to do was try to get her to become that relaxed in his own company. *All* he had to do...! That wasn't going to be so easy.

But they had made a start. He had managed to kiss her lightly a couple of times today without her jumping like a startled doe. In time he hoped they would be able to find that easy friendship that had once existed between them.

Even if being Andie's friend was the last thing he wanted to be!

Being pregnant definitely suited Andie, that nausea she had experienced initially having all but gone now, leaving her with a contented glow that made her infinitely desirable. In fact, he was going to find great difficulty in containing that desire until after their wedding in three weeks' time.

'I forgot to tell you,' he said casually as he drove her

back to her apartment later that afternoon. 'I called Jonas's office earlier too—'

'You did have a busy morning,' Andie murmured derisively, her smile totally relaxed as she looked across at him.

'It's the way I am,' he admitted ruefully. 'If something needs fixing, then do it. Now. Not later. I spoke to someone called Dorothy. Jonas's secretary, I presume—'

'And watchdog.' Andie laughed. 'Danie swears that if Dorothy hadn't approved of her she may have had a fight on her hands where marrying Jonas is concerned. She's talking nonsense, of course. It's obvious to anyone with eyes in their head that Jonas absolutely adores Danie.' She frowned wistfully.

Adam wasn't unaware of her wistfulness. As he wasn't unaware of the fact that Andie had to wish their marriage was going to be the love-match her sisters' were.

But a lot of couples had started life together on less than they had between them; there was absolutely no reason why their own marriage shouldn't be as happy and successful as Harrie and Quinn's obviously was—Danie and Jonas's too, he shouldn't wonder.

He reached out and briefly touched her hand. He would make this marriage right for them. For Andie's and the baby's sake, he had to!

'Dorothy didn't seem to think there would be any problem with our seeing Jonas on Monday,' he continued lightly.

Andie quirked teasing brows in his direction. 'The Munroe influence wins out again!'

'Actually—' he grinned '—it was the Summer influence this time! It seems that, as Danie's sister, you come in for preferential treatment where Jonas Noble is concerned.'

Andie snorted. 'I told you Dorothy is in charge!'

Adam didn't particularly care who made the decisions,

as long as he got to share this pregnancy with Andie. 'We have an appointment to see Jonas at two o'clock on Monday. Apparently he isn't usually available on Monday afternoons, but for you he'll make the exception.'

Andie nodded. 'Jonas runs a free clinic twice a week for women who need his professional help but can't afford to pay for it.'

Adam felt himself bristle with resentment at the undoubted admiration for the other man in Andie's tone. He had met Jonas Noble at the wedding a couple of weeks ago, had found him charming enough. But, knowing how difficult Danie could be on occasion, Adam didn't doubt the other man had a lot more to him than that surface charm. He just didn't like the fact that Andie obviously thought so too!

'We can have lunch together again, if that suits you,' Adam said stiffly. 'And then go on to the clinic.'

She paused. 'I can't think of anything else I have to do on Monday. Or any other day, for that matter,' she muttered, obviously alluding to the fact that she was no longer working, her diary remarkably empty after years of being tied to a tight working and social schedule.

'Try to keep three weeks on Saturday free, too, hmm?' he teased.

'I'll try.' She laughed huskily, obviously mellowed by the success of their engagement luncheon.

And it had been a success, the others taking their cue from Adam, and treating their engagement and impending marriage with all the excitement it should have. There had even been a couple of jokes about two matrons of honour; Harrie was sure that Danie wouldn't want to be left out.

After years of putting any thoughts of marriage from his own mind, Adam found he was quite looking forward to the wedding in three weeks' time too. Andie was going to be his wife, and that was something he had never thought would happen!

'Would you like to come to dinner this evening?' Andie offered as they reached her apartment, Adam having already reluctantly explained that he would have to at least show his face in his own office this afternoon. Reluctantly because, now that Andie had agreed to marry him, he found he didn't want to let her out of his sight!

'You mean you can cook, too?' he said with mock— surprise.

Andie's eyes gleamed in the confines of the parked car. '"Too"?'

'You make love rather beautifully,' he told her.

Her gaze no longer met his, heated colour in her cheeks now. 'Don't patronise me, Adam,' she said. 'I was awkward and inexperienced.'

'You could never be awkward in anything you do, Andie.' He reached out and gently touched one of her hot cheeks. 'And you were lovely in your inexperience. I'm only sorry—'

'I have to go, Adam,' she announced abruptly, reaching out to open her car door before getting out onto the pavement. 'Don't get out,' she said as he would have done exactly that, bending down to speak to him. 'I'm making dinner for seven-thirty, if you would care to join me.'

Too far, too soon, Adam acknowledged heavily as he drove away. Obviously that night was still something Andie would rather not talk about. Even if she now carried the physical proof of that night inside her.

But he wished she had let him finish saying how part of him wished he could have given her the same gift she had given him that night three months ago, that his own experience hadn't far outweighed her own. There was nothing he could do to change it now, but how he now regretted all those other relationships that had meant nothing to him.

The last thing he wanted, or needed, after the enjoyable lunch with Andie and her family, was to see that familiar figure waiting for him outside his office.

Not here.

Not now, he wanted to cry.

The woman arched an eyebrow. 'You don't look pleased to see me, Adam,' she said.

He was never pleased to see her. How could he be?

'Aren't you going to invite me in, Adam?' she demanded as someone brushed past them in the corridor on their way to the office further down.

She knew, damn her, that the last thing he wanted was for anyone to see him talking to her. To add two and two together, and come up with—

'I suppose you had better,' he rasped, pushing open the outer door, nodding tersely to Andrew, his assistant, as he walked straight past him and through into his own office.

All the time knowing she would be following him. He could hear the softness of her breathing, smell her perfume.

That perfume. He had smelt it in his sleep for years. Until Andie's perfume had replaced it...!

He sat down behind his desk, eyes steely grey, totally unmoved by the faded beauty this woman had become. 'What do you want?'

She tilted her head, giving him a considering look. 'There's something different about you...' she commented thoughtfully.

Adam felt himself stiffen. How could she tell! How did she know? Had just the thought of having Andie for his wife really made him look different?

Because if it had he would have to do everything in his power to hide that difference from this woman. At least until three weeks on Saturday. When his marriage to Andie would be a *fait accompli*.

When this woman could no longer do or say anything to change that!

CHAPTER EIGHT

THERE was something different about Adam this evening.

Andie had noticed that difference as soon as he'd arrived shortly before seven-thirty to join her for dinner at her apartment. For one thing there had been no smile on his face. And for another, he hadn't even attempted to kiss her hello...

Strange how she had already become used to those light kisses of his, and how much she had missed that casual intimacy this evening.

She watched him below lowered lashes as they ate the avocado and prawns with marie-rose sauce she had prepared for their first course. Adam ate the food automatically, not even seemingly aware of what he was eating. Although he complimented her on the choice once his plate was empty.

Andie removed the plates, looking down at him thoughtfully. 'What did you just eat?'

Adam blinked up at her. 'I—well—it was prawns and—and something, wasn't it?' he said falteringly.

'And something,' she agreed, becoming more and more convinced that Adam's thoughts were definitely elsewhere.

Unless he had finally realised that they were going to be married in a matter of weeks, that they would spend a lot of their evenings together like this...?

'I'll go and get the second course,' she announced abruptly.

'We'll go and get the second course,' Adam told her decisively as he stood up. 'I have no problem with eating

111

at home, but I do object to having you wait on me.' He followed her out to the kitchen.

Despite the fact that Andie had known this man for most of her life, she realised that they really knew very little about each other's private lives. For one thing, she had no idea whether Adam usually ate at home in the evenings, or whether he went out to a restaurant. There was no doubting the fact that he could afford to do the latter if he chose to, but restaurant food, although enjoyable, could become tiresome on a regular basis.

At least, that was what she told herself as she served the lamb chops, baby potatoes and peas that were their main course, knowing she had only provided cheeses to follow.

Maybe she was expecting too much of Adam. Maybe it was a little early in their new relationship to be bombarding him with domesticity!

The thing was, she actually quite enjoyed cooking, although it was her sister Danie who was the trained cook. Amongst other things.

'I hope you like lamb,' Andie said awkwardly as she served the sauce to go with it.

'I'll eat anything,' Adam replied distractedly. 'Sorry—I didn't mean that quite the way it sounded.' He groaned as he realised what he had just said. 'I'm sure the meal is going to be just fine,' he added reassuringly.

She frowned across at him. 'Adam—'

'Would you like me to open the wine?' he prompted, holding up the bottle that stood on the side, his expression once again unreadable.

She had forgotten all about serving the wine earlier! Not that she would drink any herself, but she had put out a nice bottle of red wine for Adam to enjoy—and promptly forgotten all about it.

She knew why she had, of course; Adam's distant behaviour when he'd arrived having thrown her into a state of confusion...

In fact, this evening wasn't going at all as she had thought it would. They had seemed so relaxed with each other earlier today, the engagement lunch with most of her family a complete success.

She had been touched that Adam had gone to so much trouble on her behalf, and this evening's meal came in the form of a thank-you for that thoughtfulness. But since his arrival half an hour ago Adam had given every impression that this was the last place he wanted to be.

Was she the last person he wanted to be with?

Well, what else had she expected? Until a few days ago, Adam hadn't even thought about having a wife, let alone taking on a baby as well. She had been in shock herself for weeks after realising she was pregnant, had denied it to herself for the same amount of time; it was going to take Adam time to get used to this idea too...

'I hope you don't mind if I opt for an early night once we've had our meal.' She spoke brightly once they were seated back at the dining-table. 'It's been rather an—exciting day, one way or another,' she said with a rueful glance at the engagement ring that twinkled and glittered on her left hand.

Adam's ring. A ring she had thought never to own.

She had dreamt of one day being with Adam. Of course she had. She couldn't be in love with him and not have her dreams. But those dreams had involved Adam realising that he was in love with her too, that he wanted to spend the rest of his life with her. Even in her wildest dreams she had never envisaged being with him under these circumstances!

Adam paused in the act of sipping his red wine, giving

her a sharp look. 'You're feeling okay, aren't you? Today hasn't been too much for you?'

Poor Adam; he was the one who had found today too much!

'Not at all,' she reassured him soothingly. 'I just tire easily still. Jonas assures me that soon I'm going to blossom with vitality and good health,' she added dryly. 'I keep waiting for the day!'

There was no answering smile on Adam's face. 'I'll feel better myself once I've spoken to him on Monday.'

She shrugged. 'He isn't going to tell you much more than I already have. I was nauseous to the point of incapacity to begin with,' she recalled with a grimace. 'But that's mainly passed,' she added quickly as she saw Adam's dark frown. 'There really is no problem with the pregnancy, Adam.' She reached out and lightly touched his hand, hastily removing it again when she felt the tingling sensation that ran heatedly up her arm.

Adam still looked grim. 'So you keep telling me. I'll just feel better once Jonas has confirmed that for me.'

Andie looked at him beneath lowered lashes. 'I hope you aren't going to be an over-protective father-to-be,' she remonstrated playfully.

Adam gave up any pretence of eating the lamb, carefully placing his knife and fork on the plate before looking across at her. 'I'm sorry.' He indicated the half-eaten food. 'I think I'm still full from lunch.'

Andie believed that, for the moment, he had taken as much of the Summer family as he could take. But especially her and their baby...

'Me too.' She put down her own cutlery and stood up, unaware of the fact that she was nervously twisting her engagement ring round and round her finger. 'I really am rather tired, Adam...' she told him, her nerves stretched out almost to breaking point now.

She had thought earlier, when they'd chosen the rings together, during the lunch with her family, that perhaps this was going to work out after all. But alone with Adam like this, with him so obviously finding the situation such a strain, she wasn't so sure...

'Of course.' He nodded abruptly. 'I—let's go back to the sitting-room for a while, hmm? I know you're tired, but it is only eight-fifteen.'

Though the last hour, since his arrival, had seemed more like eight!

'We still have a few things to discuss,' he said gruffly.

Andie stiffened warily, making no effort to move into the sitting-room, as he suggested. 'Such as?'

'Such as where we're going to live once we're married, for one thing,' he pointed out.

She stopped to think. Where they were going to live? Why, London, of course. Her own work was here, and, although Adam travelled extensively in his work as a film producer, his office was based here. Besides, as they all knew in the Summer family, Adam hated the countryside, had never made any secret of the fact that visiting the family there was something of a chore. She didn't understand what he meant about where they would live once they were married. Maybe they did have things to discuss, after all...

'Perhaps we should go through to the sitting-room,' she agreed.

'I'll make us some coffee. You can still drink coffee, can't you?' Adam paused on his way to the kitchen.

'I can now,' she acknowledged distractedly, still thinking as she followed him into the kitchen with their used plates. 'You don't know where anything is,' she explained at his questioning look.

'I can find it.' He took a firm hold of her shoulders and turned her back towards the sitting-room. 'You've done enough for one day,' he declared as he gave her a gentle push towards the adjoining room.

She might have done, but the next few minutes alone in the sitting-room, still with only her thoughts, was something she could have done without at the moment.

No one had said this was going to be easy, she told herself impatiently. As long as she and Adam at last kept talking they should be all right.

'This is good,' she said to him once she had sipped the strong coffee he had just made.

'Don't sound so surprised.' He smiled, stretching out his own length in the chair opposite hers. 'A man who has lived on his own for as long as I have should at least have learnt how to make good coffee!'

She swallowed hard, wondering if that were the point here; a man who had lived on his own for as long as Adam had...

She moistened dry lips. 'Adam—'

'Don't take that comment any further than it was meant,' he said astutely. 'I'm sure you're as aware as I am that living alone isn't all it's made out to be.' He looked at her with narrowed grey eyes.

Of course she was aware of that. Sometimes the hours she wasn't working could be too lonely, the silence in her apartment too heavy and still. But she had always had the Summer estate to return to if she felt in the need of company. As had Adam himself...

'But—'

'No buts, Andie. I've lived on my own most of my life,' he explained grimly. 'And I'm sure you're going to find I have some annoying habits, such as leaving the bathroom untidy, or squeezing the toothpaste from the middle rather than the bottom of the tube—'

'I always use the dispenser type myself,' she put in quickly.

'You see,' Adam rejoined. 'That's one problem solved already.'

But, like Adam, she realised it was a minor one in comparison with some of the others they were going to come up against. Such as where they were going to live!

'I'm sure we're both going to have to make adjustments,' she accepted.

'But...?' he guessed.

'Where do you want to live once we're married?' she asked guardedly.

'In a house. With a garden,' he came back unhesitantly. 'And preferably somewhere our son or daughter can breathe fresh air,' he added.

Andie was taken aback. Adam hated the country, had always been extremely vocal on the subject. What—?

'I want our child to have the things I didn't,' he continued flatly, his expression remote. 'Air to breathe. A garden to play in. Trees to climb.'

Presents on birthdays and at Christmas...

Oh, how she wished she knew more about Adam's early life. But from an early age she had been told by her mother that she was never to intrude in that part of Adam's life, that if he ever wanted her, or any of the sisters, to know, he would tell them. He never had.

Would it still be intruding, as his future wife, to ask him about it...?

Andie was looking at him as if she had never seen him before. And he couldn't exactly blame her.

She had accepted his proposal, was obviously trying to

make the best of the fact that the two of them were soon to be married, but it wasn't what she had planned for her life, was it? Harrie and Danie both had careers too, very responsible ones, but Andie had always been the sister who put her work before everything else. It was the existence of their baby that had put that career indefinitely on hold.

Andie had come to terms with her pregnancy, now she needed time to come to terms with becoming his wife.

'Just think about it,' Adam encouraged. 'It doesn't have to be too far out of London, can easily be in commuter distance. I just—the idea of bringing a child up in an apartment in the middle of London just doesn't appeal.' He pulled a face.

Andie still looked troubled.

Damn it, this was all his fault. If he hadn't lost his head that night. If—

If. If. If!

It was too late for ifs. He really would do everything in his power to make this marriage and motherhood as enjoyable as possible for Andie.

Well…as enjoyable as it could be when she was obviously marrying a man she didn't love.

'Andie, I have to go away tomorrow for a few days,' he decided abruptly. 'some filming in Germany has hit a few financial snags the director wants to discuss with me. I should only be away a few days.' He couldn't seem to stop talking as she just looked at him with those deep green eyes. 'Three or four at the most,' he concluded lamely.

Because until a few moments ago, he hadn't given the filming in Germany another thought, not since he'd received the director's message this afternoon. If he had thought about it at all he had been considering asking the director to come to London for discussions. Until a few moments ago…

Andie looked very much in need of some breathing space. Just space, really. From him.

And after his visitor earlier today, he needed some time to think too. Oh, not about Andie; he had no doubts where marrying Andie was concerned. She was everything he could ever want in a wife.

It was getting through the next three weeks to the wedding that was consuming most of his thoughts. If that woman got so much as a hint that he was going to be married—!

His mouth tightened angrily, grey eyes bleak. She had done her best to ruin his life once before; he would not let her have the chance to do so again. He still couldn't believe the bad luck that had made her appear back in his life today, of all days. But then again, why couldn't he believe it? The woman was his nemesis.

She didn't appear for months at a time usually; once it had been almost a year. That time he had almost convinced himself that he wouldn't see her again. Then she had appeared at his office, much as she had today, almost as if no time had passed at all since he had last seen her.

She always wanted the same thing. Money. And like a fool, because of some deeply buried memories of having once loved her, he always gave her what she came for.

He knew, now that Andie was to be his wife, one day he would have to tell her about the other woman, of what she had once been to him. But he wanted Andie already safely established as his wife before he did that.

Coward, an inner voice taunted him.

Yes, he was a coward. But if being a coward now meant he kept Andie in the future, then he would choose being a coward every time!

He sat forward in his seat, attempting a smile that he knew didn't quite come off. But how could it? He had been

churned up with conflicting emotions ever since he'd returned to his office this afternoon and found that wretched
woman there. Half of him was looking forward to having
Andie as his wife, and to being her husband, and the other
half of him was terrified, after this afternoon, that the wedding would never take place!

'I'll make sure I'm back in time for our appointment with
Jonas on Monday afternoon,' he promised.

Andie swallowed hard, her expression bland—deliberately so, it seemed to Adam. 'Of course you must go. I
understand completely. After all, it's your work.' She
smiled.

But her eyes didn't. Those beautiful sparkling green eyes
were completely emotionless.

Adam just wanted to sweep her up into his arms, tell her
everything, plead for her patience and understanding over
a situation that had caused him much heartache over the
years. But he knew he couldn't do that, that he had kept
his own counsel for too long. He had only ever spoken to
one person about Glenda, and he had known Barbara well
enough to trust that she had taken his secret to the grave
with her.

How he wished Barbara were here now!

'I really am rather tired now, Adam.' Andie spoke quietly, her gaze not quite meeting his. 'And I'm sure you
must have things to do if you intend flying to Germany
tomorrow,' she added pointedly.

He could feel the distance between them, a distance that
seemed to be widening, not lessening. He didn't know what
to do or say to stop it happening…!

'What will you do while I'm away?' he questioned,
knowing by the way her eyes widened indignantly that he
had once again said the wrong thing.

'I believe I managed to keep myself occupied before you

came into my life, Adam,' she replied scornfully. 'And that I will continue to do so,' she continued, green gaze flashing a warning.

He winced. 'I didn't mean—I was just taking an interest—I—'

He had sounded patronising! When, in reality, he was desperately trying to find some common ground between them before he took his departure. He didn't want to go away for three or four days feeling that things weren't right between them.

Andie stood up, moving to lightly stroke his arm. 'It's all right, Adam,' she told him. 'I do understand. This is going to take time to get used to. For both of us.'

His expression softened as he looked up at her. She really was so very much like Barbara. Perhaps if he just explained everything to Andie—

No!

It was a risk he dared not take. Not until after they were married, anyway. When he would have no choice.

He stood up, aware of Andie's move away from him as he did so, his smile slightly tinged with bitterness. If Andie didn't love him now, shied away from being close to him, how much more difficult was this going to be once they were married?

'I'll call you from Germany,' he said as the two of them walked to the door.

'You will?' Andie sounded doubtful.

'Of course I will.' He turned and grasped her arms, bending slightly so that he could look into the magnolia beauty of her face. 'I'll need to know that my fiancée is well,' he teased.

'Your pregnant fiancée,' Andie amended.

Implying that was the only reason he would be telephoning, to make sure that their baby, rather than Andie herself, was still well!

Adam wanted to assure her that it was her he cared about, her health and welfare that concerned him. But he knew she wouldn't believe him even if he tried to tell her that. Because without the existence of that baby, Andie would never have agreed to marry him...

The next three weeks, until he could make Andie his wife, stretched out before him like a minefield. And each step he took could be the one that made his future with Andie blow up in his face...!

CHAPTER NINE

'THIS is what you've always wanted, isn't it?' Harrie asked indulgently as Andie paraded in front of her in yet another wedding dress.

Andie pulled a face. 'To find a wedding dress that hides the fact I'll be almost four months pregnant when I walk down the aisle on Rome's arm as the blushing bride?'

'Good try, Andie,' her sister replied. 'But you know very well that isn't what I'm referring to.'

Of course she knew. But had she really been that transparent in her feelings towards Adam? She had thought, over the years, that she had hidden them rather well. But not, it seemed, from her eldest sister, who knew her so well...

Harrie had telephoned her yesterday and suggested the two of them went shopping today to look for a wedding dress, and, feeling Adam's absence in Germany as deeply as she was, Andie had been only too happy for the suggested diversion from her own troubled thoughts.

Adam had telephoned her yesterday evening, as he had promised he would, but their conversation had been stilted and brief, Adam finally giving her the name and telephone number of his hotel in Berlin, in case she should need to contact him over the weekend. Andie knew it was a telephone number she would never use.

She blandly met Harrie's affectionate gaze. 'I don't think I've ever given marriage too much thought, either,' she said truthfully. Mainly, because she had never been able to envisage marrying the man she loved!

123

'You're being deliberately obtuse, Andie,' her sister commented.

Andie sighed, giving up all pretence of studying this latest silk and satin wedding dress in the full-length mirror provided. 'Harrie, I'm sure you must have realised at the engagement luncheon that this isn't exactly a love—'

'I think I preferred the cream satin,' Harrie cut in, turning to the assistant who had just entered the large private fitting-room. 'My sister would like to fit the cream satin again,' she told the other woman lightly.

'Of course, Mrs McBride.' The middle-aged woman smiled politely before leaving in search of the cream dress.

Harrie grinned. 'I still get a delicious thrill down my spine every time someone calls me that!'

Mrs Munroe. Mrs Adam Munroe. Yes, Andie felt a similar thrill at the thought of being Adam's wife.

'It will all work out, you know,' Harrie continued, watching her intensely.

Andie gave her a sharp look. 'Will it?'

Harrie stood up, moving to put her arms about Andie and give her a hug. 'Adam is a kind and considerate man.' She held Andie at arm's length.

She swallowed hard. 'I know that. It's just—'

'I don't think this is the place to talk about this,' Harrie warned as the assistant returned with the requested wedding dress. 'We'll go and have some tea somewhere once we've finished here, hmm?' She gave Andie's arms an understanding squeeze before moving away.

The cream satin dress, with its Empire line that did much to hide her pregnancy, was beautiful, Andie agreed a few minutes later, the choice of matching veil and satin shoes much easier to make.

'We'll go back to my house for tea,' Harrie decided as

they stepped into a waiting taxi. 'It will be much more private there.'

Andie wasn't sure she wanted to have a private chat with Harrie. Her sister knew her far too well, was sure to get the truth of this sudden engagement out of her without too much trouble.

Harrie observed Andie as they waited for the tea things to be brought through to her luxuriously comfortable sitting-room. 'You look as if you're sitting in the waiting room of the dentist—or, in your case, doctor!' she commented affectionately.

Andie knew she looked far from relaxed as she perched on the edge of one of Harrie's armchairs. But she and Adam had an agreement, and confiding the truth to her sister was not part of that agreement.

'Are you missing him very much?' Harrie prompted softly.

Strangely, yes, she was. Her life so far had been one of independence, making her own decisions, answerable to no one. Yet, in a very short time, Adam's absence, even for a few days, had left a huge gulf in her life…

'Don't answer that; I can see that you are,' Harrie told her as the tea things were brought in and placed on the table between them. 'Andie, I'm not going to pry,' she assured once they were alone again. 'Your relationship with Adam is your own affair, and no one else's. Not even a big sister's! I do have one thing I want to say to you, though…'

'I thought you might have.' Andie sighed, accepting her cup of tea.

Her sister shook her head, dark hair loose around her shoulders. 'I doubt it's anything like you think it is,' she said gently. 'It's something Quinn said to me a week after we were married.'

Andie smiled. She liked and approved of her brother-in-law.

Harrie nodded. 'He was almost Adam's age when we got married, and I wondered—stupidly, as it turned out—whether he would regret it, whether he would long for his freedom, resent the ties of marriage—'

'But Quinn loves you!' Andie protested.

Her sister shrugged. 'He had still been a bachelor for almost forty years. But when I said those things to him, do you know what his reply was...?'

Andie couldn't even begin to guess. Just as she didn't see what bearing this had on her impending marriage to Adam.

Harrie sipped her tea before answering. 'Quinn told me that men of his age do not marry unless they are absolutely sure they're doing the right thing—that they are marrying the right person,' she qualified.

Andie gave another humourless smile. 'That doesn't exactly apply in this case, does it?' she said in reply.

Her sister looked sympathetic. 'Well, of course, I realise that story about the two of you dating in secret isn't true—we've always been close, Andie; you would have told me if you were seeing Adam. But that doesn't change the fact that it's Adam's baby you're expecting. Or that you are marrying the person you love.' She looked challengingly across at Andie.

She sighed. 'And Adam?'

'He wouldn't marry you either if he didn't feel you could both make a success of it,' Harrie said with certainty.

'But he doesn't love me!' Andie heard herself groan, the relief of at last being able to talk to someone about this surprise engagement and hasty marriage proving too much for her. 'He's only marrying me because of the baby.'

Harrie looked startled momentarily. 'Has he said that...?'

Andie avoided her sister's compassionate gaze. She-did-not-want-to-cry. If she started, she might not be able to stop!

'He doesn't need to.' She shook her head. 'I—he—he's in love with someone else!' The words came out in a flood, as quickly shocking her into silence as she heard their stark reality.

She had told herself that she wouldn't think of Adam's feelings for her mother, that it could only lead to unhappiness. But, without Adam's confident support, those doubts had set in once again.

Harrie looked at her with assessing eyes. 'Are you sure?'

Andie easily remembered Adam's devastation when her mother had died, his continued bachelor state as the years had passed. 'Oh, yes, I'm sure.'

Close as she was to both her sisters, Adam's feelings for her mother were something she had never discussed with either of them. It had somehow seemed disloyal. To her mother—because she knew, fond as her mother had been of Adam, that she had not returned his feelings, that she had been totally in love with Rome. And to Adam—because it had been a futile love that must have caused him deep pain over the years.

Her sister stood up. 'I don't believe it, Andie. I've seen the way Adam looks at you—'

'Well, he doesn't find me unattractive, if that's what you mean!' She put her arms protectively about the slight swelling that was their child.

'It isn't,' Harrie said reprovingly. 'You were always his favourite. When we were all little—'

'Harrie, you're talking about twenty years ago,' she interrupted wearily. 'We're big girls now—remember?'

Her sister paused. 'He has to have remained a bachelor all these years for a reason.'

'And you think I'm it?' Andie asked incredulously.

'I think it's a possibility,' Harrie said slowly.

She shouldn't have spoken, should never have confided her doubts to her sister, could see that Harrie was really worried now. If Harrie became worried enough, then she would discuss this with their father. If Rome got in on the act...!

Andie made a concerted effort to erase the frown from between her eyes, her expression altogether brighter as she gave a slightly self-conscious laugh. 'I think I'm having a touch of wedding nerves,' she excused lightly.

Harrie gave her a searching look, but Andie managed to meet that gaze unwaveringly. She shouldn't have said anything, should never have voiced her fears to Harrie. Because Harrie had always been the big protective sister, and her own marriage to Quinn hadn't changed that.

'A husband and a baby!' Andie reflected. 'Is it any wonder I'm panicking?'

'No...'

But Harrie still wasn't convinced!

She laughed softly. 'Didn't you have any nerves before you and Quinn were married?'

'I've just told you that I did...' Harrie still looked serious.

'I'll be fine once Adam is back home again,' Andie told her decisively. 'I miss him, that's all.'

And, surprisingly, she did. How quickly he had become a part of her life, and how easily those doubts set in when his physical presence wasn't here to reassure her!

'I had better go now.' She picked up her shoulder-bag. 'He said he would ring me this evening.'

'It's only five o'clock,' Harrie teased.

'He may try and ring me before he goes out this evening,' Andie insisted determinedly.

In fact, she knew it was doubts about what Adam was actually doing in Germany that had fuelled her uncertainties. They had agreed they would be faithful in their marriage to each other—but they weren't married yet! With the sudden way Adam's circumstances had changed, he could have a few loose ends in his life to tie up. A few women he had to break the sad news to!

Although he sounded cheerful enough when he rang her at seven o'clock. Early enough to still allow him to go out to dinner?

Stop this, Andie, she told herself firmly. She had never been jealous in her life—and she wasn't about to start now!

'I'm coming home tomorrow,' he told her cheerfully. 'Do you feel like meeting me at the airport?'

He was coming home a day earlier than expected! She was so thrilled by this news that she almost missed what he had said next. Almost...

'You want me to meet you off the plane?' she said uncertainly.

'Well, only if you want to. Of course, it's a long way to go. And you probably have other plans. Forget I even suggested—'

'What time does your plane land?' she cut in excitedly. Adam wanted her to meet him at the airport! Which meant he was coming back alone.

One of her imaginings in the last couple of days Adam had been away was that this business trip was perhaps a little too convenient, that perhaps Adam had taken someone else away with him, with the idea of softening the blow when he told the woman of his impending marriage. As far as she was aware Adam had never been seriously involved in any of the relationships he had indulged in over the years. But if there were someone in his life at the moment... He wasn't cruel either.

However, if he wanted her to meet him at the airport...!

'Some time in the afternoon,' he supplied distractedly. 'But it was a stupid idea, Andie. An hour's journey out to the airport, the stuffy atmosphere there. And then I could be delayed—'

'I'll be there, Adam,' she declared, knowing she needed to see him. If only to reassure herself he really was going to be her husband.

'You will...?'

She almost laughed at his own uncertainty. But she didn't. Because she had a feeling Adam was as insecure in their present relationship as she was. Hopefully it would be different once they were married.

'I will,' she told him steadfastly. 'I'll be the one that slightly resembles a balloon!'

Adam laughed softly. 'You look absolutely beautiful—and you know it!'

She knew no such thing. But if Adam thought so, that was all that mattered. 'I'll see you tomorrow afternoon,' she assured him before ringing off.

Now get a grip, Andie Summer, she told herself. She was one of the Summer sisters, Jerome Summer's youngest daughter, had never lacked for confidence in her life.

And she couldn't start now.

Adam felt like a giddy schoolboy. Anticipation tinged with excitement. And all because Andie was going to be waiting at the airport for him.

He wasn't sure what had prompted him to suggest she meet him off the plane. In all the years he had been travelling all over the world, for pleasure as well as work, there had never been anyone waiting for him to arrive home before.

But now he had Andie. His fiancée. Shortly to be his wife. How good that sounded!

His had been a relatively lonely life, the Summer family the closest he had ever come to having one of his own. But now he would have a wife. And shortly a child too. He had never realised before how good it felt to belong with someone, to someone.

Which made Andie and their child all the more precious...

No, he wouldn't think of Glenda today, wouldn't let her spoil this for him. As she had spoilt so many things in the past.

Andie looked absolutely gorgeous as she waited in Arrivals for him; her hair was an abundance of loose gold curls, just as he liked to see it, green eyes sparkling, her face flushed and beautiful. So much so that he noticed several other men looking at her admiringly.

He scowled darkly as he caught, and held, the gaze of one of those men, grey eyes communicating a warning; Andie was his!

'Adam?'

He turned back to find that Andie had walked over to join him, looking up at him questioningly. He forced himself to relax, putting down his case and briefcase to sweep her up into his arms and give her a lingering kiss.

'Wow,' she murmured throatily as they broke the kiss but still stood in each other's arms. 'Perhaps you should go away more often, Adam.'

He had decided, during the long dragging hours in Germany, that he wouldn't go away in future at all if Andie couldn't go with him. He had missed her too much.

His arms tightened briefly before he released her. 'No more travelling until after we're married, at least.' And even then it was questionable; Andie's advancing preg-

nancy meant that she probably wouldn't be able to fly anywhere within a matter of weeks.

He looked down at the small case and briefcase, cursing
the fact that he wouldn't have a hand free to hold Andie's
hand; he wanted to keep this closeness between them, had
missed her more than he had thought it possible to miss
anyone.

Andie solved that particular problem by picking up his
briefcase for him, smiling at him companionably as he
linked his hand with hers, the two of them walking outside
into the autumn sunshine.

It felt good to be alive, Adam decided happily.

'Where shall we go for our honeymoon?' He turned to
Andie as she drove the two of them back into London.

She looked surprised. 'I didn't know we were going to
have one.'

Adam had thought of little else but having Andie as his
wife while he'd been away. In fact, he had probably agreed
to all that film director's demands simply so that he could
get back to Andie as quickly as possible! Their honeymoon,
having Andie completely to himself for a few days, had
been paramount in those thoughts...

'Oh, I think we should, don't you?'

'If you can spare the time.'

Not exactly enthusiastic, but then it was still early days
between them. 'As we're only going to do this once, I think
the least we owe ourselves is a honeymoon,' he said firmly.

'I'm told that Paris is the place for honeymoons,' Andie
murmured huskily.

'Then Paris it shall be,' he decided. 'Leave all the arrangements to me.'

Andie tilted her head as she turned briefly to look at him.
'You like organising things, don't you?'

Adam shrugged, not altogether sure of her reason for the

statement. 'It's certainly a fact that if I didn't organise things in my own life then they would never get done.'

'Hmm.'

His eyes narrowed. 'What does that mean?'

'"Hmm"?' Andie repeated mildly.

'Yes—"hmm"!'

It was Andie's turn to shrug. 'I'm pretty used to making arrangements for myself too.'

He was overstepping an invisible line by choosing to make all their decisions for them! Andie hadn't exactly said that, but it was obvious what she meant. Adam foresaw some delicate manoeuvring between them over the next few months, while they adjusted to each other. Oh, well, no one had told him marriage was easy. In fact, he knew it wasn't!

'We'll make the Paris arrangements together,' he amended.

Andie laughed softly. 'Did that hurt?'

He gave a self-deriding grin. 'Not too badly, no,' he acknowledged, looking around them. 'You know where my apartment is, don't you?' They had reached the city, but his apartment was in the opposite direction to the one in which Andie was driving.

'I know where it is,' she conceded slowly. 'I just wasn't sure where you wanted to go.'

'Home. So that I can wash the travel dust off me.' He grimaced. 'There's something particularly—dirty, about air travel. I always get off the plane feeling as if I need a shower!'

'I went out with Harrie yesterday and bought my wedding dress,' Andie told him suddenly.

'You mentioned that on the telephone last night,' he reminded her watching her carefully.

They were talking for the sake of it, he realised. Trivial

conversation. Because they were both wary of it becoming a serious one…?

Or was it the thought of coming to his apartment with him that was making Andie seem so distant suddenly?

Close as his relationship had been with all the Summer family over the years, only Rome had actually ever visited him at his apartment. There had never been any reason for any of the three sisters to go there.

Until now.

He reached out and lightly stroked Andie's hair, knowing by the way she flinched that things were still far from relaxed between them. The kiss they had shared at the airport had given him hope that—

It was the thought of going to his apartment that was now making Andie so jumpy!

'Perhaps you would like to make us both some coffee?' he suggested once they had arrived in his penthouse apartment. 'It will give me time to hide the whips and chains!'

Andie had been looking curiously around at her surroundings, but she turned to him sharply at this last comment.

'I'm joking, Andie!' he assured her exasperatedly as he lightly grasped her arms. 'You've looked as if you expect me to pounce on you at any second ever since I suggested we come here. I thought the mention of the whips and chains might confirm all your worst fears about the man you've decided to marry.'

'Very funny,' she snapped.

Adam grinned. 'Disappointed?'

'Not in the least,' she said. 'I'm just a beginner—remember?'

Oh, yes, he remembered. Every creamy, untouched inch of her. It kept him awake at night remembering!

Adam released her arms to hold her gently against him.

So am I when it comes to you,' he whispered huskily. 'I ache with wanting you, Andie!'

She gave him a startled look. 'You do?'

His answer was to pull her even closer, knowing the physical evidence of his desire must be obvious—even to a beginner!

Andie looked confused before turning away. 'I'll make the coffee while you take a shower.'

He laughed at the blush in her cheeks, slowly releasing her. 'That's probably the safest plan—although not the one I would personally have opted for!'

'Audrey told Rome that anticipation of their wedding night is good for him,' Andie observed.

'Good for her,' he replied approvingly. 'I—' He broke off as the telephone began to ring, frowning darkly. Who the hell could be telephoning him at this time on a Sunday?

Very few people actually had his private telephone number, which limited the identity of the caller to a handful of people. And at least one of them was someone he did not want to talk to in front of Andie...

'Shouldn't you answer that?' She eyed the ringing telephone.

'Officially I'm not here,' he denied, his expression grim. His relationship with Andie was still too tenuous to risk answering that call.

'But—'

'There, it's stopped now,' he said with relief as the telephone suddenly went silent. 'I'll take that shower, and then we can decide where we would like to go for dinner.'

'And if the phone rings again?' Andie prompted softly.

He drew in a ragged breath. 'Don't answer it.'

She looked at him searchingly for several long seconds before going to the room he had told her was the kitchen.

Damn, Adam muttered to himself as he stripped off in

his bedroom in preparation of taking his shower in the adjoining bathroom.

Andie, he knew, had drawn her own conclusions about his refusal to answer the telephone call. While he might not like having her believe it was another woman, someone he was—or, now that the two of them were to be married, had been!—involved with, he knew that the truth was even less acceptable.

Three weeks, until the wedding, that was all he asked. Then he would have to tell Andie everything...

CHAPTER TEN

'SOMEHOW I was expecting that to be cold,' Andie said with some surprise.

Jonas smiled at her as he continued to smooth the clear-warm-gel over her bare abdomen. 'I like to make this as pleasant an experience as possible for you mothers-to-be!'

Andie knew she was talking for the sake of it. But it hadn't occurred to her, when they had made this appointment to see Jonas, that he would suggest doing an ultrasound scan for them, so that they could actually see the baby inside her on what was the equivalent of a television screen.

She was talking because she felt embarrassed at being naked from sternum to thighs in front of the watching Adam!

It had been different the night they had made love, emotions and passion high. Just as it hadn't seemed the same thing at all when he'd come upon her sunbathing in her bikini in Majorca. Actually lying here on the medical bed, baring the slight swell of her tummy, somehow felt very intimate. Even with Jonas present!

Jonas hadn't seemed in the least surprised that it was Adam, a man he had met only briefly before, who had accompanied Andie on this visit as the baby's father. Danie and Jonas had arrived back from their honeymoon yesterday, and Andie could only assume that they had seen Rome and he had told them of the wedding in three weeks' time. No doubt Danie would have something to say—to both of them!—when they next saw her!

137

Jonas sat back, smiling at Andie before looking across her to where Adam sat on her other side. 'Are you ready for this?' he prompted gently.

Andie suddenly felt extremely nervous. What if she were mistaken? If Jonas were mistaken? If there wasn't a baby at all? Adam wouldn't want to marry her then, and—

'We're ready.' Adam was the one to answer the other man gruffly, reaching out to tightly grasp one of Andie's hands as they lay at her sides.

'Right.' Jonas's voice was businesslike now. 'Your abdomen is ultra-sensitive at the moment, so the scanner may feel a little strange as I move it around to give you the full picture,' he warned. 'But I'm sure the end result will be worth it,' he added warmly.

Adam's hand tightened around hers, but Andie couldn't look at him, concentrating her attention on the television screen that stood beside them.

Her breath caught and held in her throat as she saw the shape of a tiny skull and body on the right-hand side of the screen. A baby. It really was there. Their baby. Hers and Adam's!

There was a definite tiny face there too; eyes, a little snub nose, and a slightly open mouth.

'My God...!' She heard Adam breath emotionally at her side.

She did turn to look at him then, her own emotions getting the better of her as she saw the tears falling unashamedly down his cheeks.

She reached out to smooth them away, her fingertips gentle against his skin.

It wasn't until Adam reached out and touched her own cheeks that she became aware of her own tears. But seeing the baby like that, so small and helpless, but so safe and secure inside her, suddenly made it all real. And so incredibly beautiful.

'Er—I hope you two are concentrating on this,' Jonas broke in lightly.

Andie and Adam shared a smile of complete intimacy before turning back towards the screen.

Just in time to see the shape of a second head and body on the left-hand side of the screen!

'What—?'

'Twins,' Jonas answered Adam calmly. 'I had my suspicions, but—well, this confirms it. There they both are.' He looked at the screen with satisfaction.

'Twins?' Andie broke out of her stupor long enough to gasp disbelievingly. 'You mean there are two of them?'

'Twins usually implies two, Andie,' Jonas teased her, freezing the picture onto the screen before removing the scanner. 'And everything present and correct, as far as I can tell.'

'But—I don't—how—are you—sure?' she finally gasped weakly; it had never occurred to her that she could be carrying more than one baby, her earlier embarrassment completely forgotten in the face of this revelation.

'Very sure,' Jonas answered confidently. 'As long as there isn't another one hiding behind these two. In which case, it's triplets.'

Andie's eyes widened 'You don't think—'

'No, I don't.' Jonas laughed softly at Andie's disbelieving gasp. 'But it briefly diverted you both from your obvious surprise that you're expecting twins!'

'I'm sure Danie appreciates your humour, Jonas,' Andie said irritably. 'But I'm not sure that we do.'

She glanced nervously at Adam. He hadn't said a word since Jonas had first shown them those two tiny human beings on the screen, that picture frozen there now, totally indisputable.

'I'm going to leave the two of you alone with your children for a few minutes,' Jonas told them, obviously aware of how emotional all this was for them both. 'Let you become acquainted with each other. I still need to do some more scanning before you leave, but I can come back and do that in a few minutes.' When you've both got over your shock, his tone implied. 'And you'll be able to take some photographs away with you when you leave,' he added warmly.

Neither of them noticed, Andie was sure, when Jonas stood up to leave, they just heard the closing of the door behind him.

Andie and Adam stared at the screen. Two babies, one on either side, facing each other.

Would they be identical? Two boys or two girls? Or could it be that they were two entirely separate entities, a boy and a girl? No doubt Jonas would be able to tell them that, too, if she were willing to have a test. But did Andie really want to know? More to the point, did Adam?

She turned slowly to look at him, to find his own eyes still fixed on the screen. The tears had stopped falling now, but his eyes had taken on a silver sheen where moisture still gathered there.

'I can't—it's—they're ours, Andie!' Adam suddenly ground out possessively, his hand tightly gripping hers now. 'I never imagined I would ever have one child, let alone two!'

'Do you mind?' Andie voiced her uncertainty. After all, he had never envisaged being married, let alone being presented with a ready-made family several months later.

He looked at her steadily. 'Do you?'

She glanced back at those two tiny creatures on the

screen, a flow of maternal love already reaching out to them both. 'No, of course I don't,' she denied fiercely.

'Neither do I,' he assured her with emotion. 'It's like Christmas and Easter all rolled into one!'

But not those barren Christmases, Easters, and birthdays he had known as a child. Perhaps, only perhaps, their children would help to alleviate some of that awful loneliness he had known then. She hoped so!

She gave a shaky smile. 'I can't imagine how this could have happened. There are no twins in my family, and— What is it, Adam?' She became concerned as she saw the way his mouth suddenly tightened grimly.

'Nothing,' he muttered. 'Absolutely nothing.'

But Andie wasn't convinced. It was—something. 'Do you have twins in your family?' she asked, aware that he didn't like talking about his family.

The two of them had made a list of people they wanted to invite to the wedding as they'd lingered over dinner the evening before. Not one of the names Adam had given her had appeared to be a member of his own family. Knowing how sensitive he was on the subject, Andie hadn't questioned it; after all, it was up to Adam who he wanted as guests at his own wedding.

He released her hand, standing up abruptly to walk over to stare out of the window, although there was no way he could actually see anything; the glass frosted so that no one could peer in.

'Adam?'

His shoulders hunched defensively, but he didn't turn to face her. 'I didn't think. But—yes, there have been twins in my family,' he finally confirmed unhelpfully.

Andie watched the tenseness of his back, sensing that he wasn't about to add anything to that statement. But there was no reason why he should, she decided. This was here and now and the two of them were expecting two wonderful babies.

'Adam…?' She reached out a hand to him, relieved when he turned and saw it, crossing the room in two strides to stand by the bed tightly gripping that hand. 'I can't wait to see Rome's face when we tell him, can you?' she said mischievously, determined not to let any sort of dampener fall on the magic of this incredible day.

Some of the tension left Adam as he smiled. 'You do realise that if they're two girls, he's never going to forgive us?'

Andie grinned at the thought. 'I'll just suggest that it isn't too late for him and Audrey to have a son of their own.'

Adam chuckled, shaking his head. ''You, my dear, have a decidedly wicked streak! Even if it's true,'' he added slowly. ''How would you feel about that?''

''Absolutely fine,'' she replied unhesitantly, knowing that Harrie and Danie would feel the same way. After all, why shouldn't Audrey want a child of her own?

Andie smiled, mainly with relief that the brief moment of tension between herself and Adam was completely dispelled. She would make sure it never returned. If Adam ever wanted to talk to her about his family, then he would do it in his own way and time; she wouldn't press him.

'Do you think we should invite Jonas back in now?' she suggested. 'After all, this is his clinic.'

'I think I quite like Danie's Jonas,' Adam said thoughtfully.

Jonas seemed to quite like the other man too, Andie thought, as a few minutes later he explained to them both exactly what they were seeing on the screen, shaking Adam warmly by the hand before the two of them left the clinic a short time later.

'Don't tell Danie, will you?' Andie requested of Jonas excitedly. 'I want to tell her myself.'

Jonas shook his head. 'Doctor and patient confidentiality precludes that,' he assured her. 'Even if the patient is my wife's sister!' He grinned. 'Besides, your pregnancy has already made Danie broody; the fact that it's twins will send her into hyperdrive!'

Andie's eyes widened. 'Danie is broody?' Somehow she couldn't quite see her I-can-do-anything-a-man-can-do-and-probably-better sister in that particular role. But, then, she had never quite been able to envisage Danie as anyone's wife, either...

Maybe it was always that way with your own siblings, memories of your childhood together making marriage and pregnancy seem slightly unreal? Their family had certainly changed a lot—grown—in the last six months. When the twins were born it would be even larger!

'She is,' Jonas confirmed, although he didn't look particularly bothered by the fact. 'I believe Quinn is having a similar reaction from Harrie,' he continued conversationally. 'It could have something to do with the fact that their baby sister will be the first one in the family to have children of her own.'

Andie was sure that it was, Harrie and Danie were protective of her when they were all children together, that protective air still there, despite their maturity.

'By the way—' Jonas walked down the corridor with them '—have either of you seen the newspaper today?'

'I was in the office all morning,' Adam rejoined. 'Andie?'

'I'm afraid I lazed half the morning away in the bath, and then I felt too lethargic to bother going down for a newspaper,' she admitted, having lain in the bath dreaming impossible dreams—mainly that Adam would fall madly in love with her! 'Why?' She frowned up at Jonas as he held the door open for them.

'Your father put the announcement of your forthcoming marriage in the newspaper today,' Jonas told them happily.

'He did what?' Adam exclaimed.

Andie turned to look at him, a sinking feeling in her stomach as she saw the unmistakable anger in his face.

She had believed Adam had spent some of this past weekend away dealing with any loose ends that still remained from his bachelor existence, but as she looked at him now she knew there was still someone out there that Adam didn't want to read in the newspaper about his forthcoming marriage!

'Where's Danie today?' Andie changed the subject to something more neutral. 'I telephoned her earlier, but she wasn't at home.'

Jonas smiled at the mention of his wife. 'Your father needed to go up to Edinburgh today. He asked Danie to fly him up there. She left at about eight o'clock this morning. But she assures me she'll be back in time to cook us both dinner.'

'Danie has always loved flying,' Andie said.

Once again Andie knew she was talking for the sake of it. But this time it was to give Adam time to recover from the fact that Rome had announced their marriage in the newspaper. A fact that seemed to have disturbed him...

Adam wasn't listening as Andie and Jonas talked affectionately of Danie for several minutes, glad of the respite. Today was turning out one shock on top of another, he acknowledged grimly. He and Andie were having twins. Which was amazing, incredible, wonderful! And now Rome had put the announcement in the paper without consulting either of them. Which was far from wonderful...!

He forced himself to relax slightly as Andie looked at him warily. His three weeks' grace, it seemed, had been swept away by Rome's announcement, and he couldn't say he was pleased by the fact, but that was still no reason to worry Andie. Especially when she was expecting twins!

It hadn't even occurred to him when he'd learnt of Andie's pregnancy that she could be carrying two babies. In the circumstances, maybe it should have done. But it hadn't.

The two of them walked outside into the sunshine, Andie speaking after several minutes' silence. 'I'm sure Daddy thought he was doing the right thing by putting the announcement in the newspaper,' she said.

He was sure Rome had thought so too, didn't for a moment think the other had acted maliciously. Why should he have done? Rome had no idea of the tangled mess Adam's life could sometimes become. Only Barbara had known that.

'Of course he did.' Adam gave Andie a reassuring smile. 'With the amount of weddings in the Summer family needing to be announced in recent months, the newspaper editor must be rubbing his hands with glee.'

Andie grinned. 'Six months ago none of us had even thought of marriage!'

Adam took her hand in his as they walked along side by side. 'I think we should go out to celebrate tonight, don't you? Possibly with Danie and Jonas? Jonas did say that Danie will be back in time for dinner.'

Andie's smile showed that she was pleased by this suggestion. 'I think that's an excellent idea,' she confirmed. 'This way Danie may have missed out on the engagement, but she'll be the first to hear about the twins.'

Adam's stomach seemed to rise up, turn a somersault, before falling back into place again. He had seen the two babies on the screen, even had a photograph of his very own showing those two tiny beings curled up together in foetal bliss—and he still found it incredible to believe that he was going to be a father soon, not to one baby, but two.

'You really don't mind?' He looked down intently at Andie.

'Of course not,' she answered instantly.

'But it's going to be more difficult with two,' he persisted, needing to be absolutely sure that Andie was happy with the way things were. It could be disastrous if she weren't.

Andie shook her head. 'Harder work, maybe. In fact, I'm sure it will be.'

'It might make it harder for you to return to work afterwards,' he pointed out.

Andie's laugh had a slight catch in it. 'I have a feeling I won't want to go back to work! Awful, isn't it?'' She screwed her nose up endearingly.

Adam would be perfectly happy with Andie staying at home to care for their children. In fact, he would prefer it. But there was no way he would ever make that decision for her. 'Wait and see how you feel,' he advised cautiously. 'You may find you miss all that glamour after a few months.' After all, Andie had always been extremely fashion-conscious herself.

'Motherhood may not be glamourous, but I'm sure the twins will keep me more than busy. In fact, it will probably be infinitely more fun than a job that now seems frivolous and unimportant.'

'We could always employ a nanny—'

'No way,' Andie told him determinedly. 'None of us ever had a nanny, Mummy always looked after us herself, and she said that, no matter how hard and difficult it could sometimes be, it was worth it, if only in the fact that we each knew we were totally loved.' A slightly wistful look came over her beautiful face. 'She also said that no matter how many children you have there's always enough love to go round.'

Barbara would say something like that, Adam realised sadly. She would also have been overjoyed at the prospect of grandchildren.

'Do you still miss her?' Adam heard himself ask. And then wished he hadn't, as Andie's beautiful face clouded over. 'Forget I said that,' he told her hastily. 'It was a stupid question. What I suggest we do now, if you have no other plans,' he added softly, aware that he could be domineering in his decisions without actually meaning to be; he had been in charge of just his own destiny too long, it would take time to adjust to the three—no, four—of them, as a unit!

'I have no other plans, Adam,' Andie answered him, obviously fully aware of what he was endeavouring to do.

'I just have to pop back to my office to check on a contract my secretary was preparing when I left earlier, and I thought you could come with me. Once I've dealt with the contract we could perhaps go on to an estate agent and make some enquiries about houses?' He looked at Andie questioningly.

She nodded. 'That space and garden you mentioned seems all the more appealing now that we know there will be two babies and not one. A visit to an estate agent's sounds like a very good idea,' she agreed happily.

Adam felt such a sense of ecstatic happiness himself, at the thought of their future life together, that for a moment he couldn't speak. He could see the four of them now, out in the garden together, Andie laughingly happy, the two babies gurgling merrily on a blanket on the lawn.

But, as always happened when he imagined that com-

plete happiness, a shadow loomed. A dark, ugly shadow
that he wanted nowhere near his future life with Andie.

The same shadow that loomed as they approached his
offices!

Once again there was that familiar figure, patiently waiting, a newspaper tucked under one arm!

Adam didn't need to be told that Glenda had seen the
announcement. He had spoken to her only last week, dealt
with that situation—for what he had hoped at the time
would be several months; there was absolutely no reason
for Glenda to be here now, other than the fact she had seen
the marriage announcement in the newspaper she so con-
spicuously carried.

'Adam...?' Andie looked up at him uncertainly as she
seemed to sense his sudden tension.

What did he do now? He could hardly turn tail and run.
But to actually speak to Glenda, with Andie at his side, was
even more unacceptable.

Why was there never a bus to walk under when you
needed one?

CHAPTER ELEVEN

THEY had come to an abrupt halt on the pavement after getting out of Adam's car outside his offices, Adam's sudden tension a tangible thing as Andie looked up at him worriedly.

She followed his line of vision, but there was really nothing to see, just a blonde woman in a poppy-red suit, reading some notices in an office window.

But Adam was staring at the woman as if he had seen a ghost!

Andie turned back to look at the woman herself. Tall and very slender, that blonde hair resting silkily on her shoulders, she had a sensual beauty that sometimes came with age, a beauty Andie was sure men would find attractive.

That Adam had found attractive?

It suddenly occurred to Andie that this woman could be one of those loose ends she had expected Adam to deal with now that he was marrying her.

She felt tense herself now. The last thing she wanted, today of all days—the incredible news of their twins still uppermost in her feelings!—was to have to deal with one of the legion of women who had at some time been part of Adam's life!

Although it seemed, as Adam tightly gripped her arm as they slowly began to walk towards the building that housed his offices, that she was going to have little choice in the matter.

The woman had turned now, was watching their approach with speculatively narrowed eyes.

Andie instantly felt an unexplained animosity welling up inside her!

She hadn't even spoken to the other woman. She had no proof that she was someone Adam had been involved with. Nevertheless, Andie knew that she disliked the other woman intensely.

'Adam,' the woman greeted.

'Glenda,' he bit out harshly, his hand falling away from Andie's arm now.

Andie watched the two of them, swallowing hard, knowing that if Adam ever looked at her with such contempt she could want to curl up in a corner and die.

'Aren't you going to introduce me to your fiancée, Adam?' the woman Glenda said archly. 'I take it this is your future wife?' She looked speculatively at Andie.

'I'm Andrea Summer, yes,' Andie was the one to answer stiffly, reaching out to curl her fingers about Adam's hand. A hand that was surprisingly very cold. Or perhaps not so surprising; Adam looked as if he were carved out of ice at this moment.

The woman Glenda gave her a sweeping glance before turning her attention back to Adam. 'Adam...?' she said pointedly.

His expression was grim, his mouth a thin angry line, grey eyes narrowed chillingly. Andie felt a shiver down her own spine just looking at him. Although the woman Glenda seemed unperturbed by Adam's lack of welcome, smiling at him confidently...

He drew in a harshly angry breath. 'Andrea Summer. Glenda—Howarth.'

Was it her imagination, or had there been the slightest hesitation in Adam's voice before he'd stated the other woman's surname? As if he would rather not have said it!

Although Andie couldn't imagine why not. As far as she

was aware, the other woman's name meant nothing to her. Although the same obviously wasn't true of Adam...

'Mrs Howarth,' Andie responded stiltedly, actually having no idea of the other woman's married state. The too-slender hands were bare of rings, but in this day and age that didn't mean anything; lots of women chose not to wear a wedding ring.

'Miss Summer,' the other woman drawled derisively before once again turning back to Adam. 'And the wedding is to be two weeks on Saturday, I believe?'

Adam's nostrils flared as he looked at the newspaper tucked beneath the woman's arm. 'That is one of the few newspapers I know that actually print the truth,' he replied tautly.

The woman continued to smile undauntedly. 'I trust I will be receiving an invitation?' she queried.

Andie saw raw anger flare in Adam's tightly set features, that silver gaze sending out shards of light. Whoever this woman was—whatever she had once been to Adam—he obviously did not want her at their wedding!

'It's going to be a very quiet wedding.' Andie was the one to answer the other woman. And not exactly truthfully; their guest list had added up to fifty at the last count. 'With family and only a few very close friends,' she finished firmly.

Blonde brows arched. 'Really? In that case—'

'We're actually in rather a hurry, Glenda.' Adam cut her short, fingers tightening about Andie's hand. 'So if you wouldn't mind—'

'So it would seem.' The woman looked at him for several seconds before her slightly contemptuous eyes passed on to Andie.

This woman knew, or had at least guessed, that Andie was pregnant!

Andie didn't know how she was so sure the other woman knew, she just knew that she did. Because Adam had told her? Had he excused his sudden marriage by explaining that he really had little choice in the matter, that it was literally a shotgun wedding; Rome would have taken a shotgun to Adam if they weren't married and Rome recognised the baby as being the other man's!

Andie felt slightly sick, those moments of deep emotional intimacy she and Adam had shared, as they'd gazed at their babies, disappearing like a puff of smoke.

Adam was being forced into marrying her by the circumstances of his long-standing friendship with her family, her father in particular, and, no matter how much she loved Adam, she knew she must never lose sight of that fact.

She turned blindly to Adam. Blindly, because of the tears threatening to fall. Something she would not allow to happen in front of Adam, let alone this brittle, but beautiful woman.

'If you don't mind, Adam, I think I'm really too tired to bother with the estate agents today.' To her surprise her voice sounded lightly dismissive, instead of how she really felt—heartbroken! 'In fact, I think I'll return home and rest for a while if we're going out this evening with Danie and Jonas.'

Something she was no longer looking forward to, Andie acknowledged heavily. Half an hour ago the world had seemed bright and full of promises, now it only consisted of two tiny innocent beings caught at the centre of what was, after all, merely a loveless marriage! Carrying out what now seemed nothing but a charade, in front of her sister and Jonas, was going to take every ounce of courage she possessed!

'Andie—'

'I'll call Danie and Jonas later this afternoon, and let you know where and at what time we're meeting them for dinner,' Andie pushed smoothly into what she knew was going to be Adam's protest at having her cut their afternoon together short like this. She did it with all of her old authority; she was perfectly capable of choosing to make decisions without consulting Adam first! 'I'll leave you to talk to Mrs Howarth, Adam.'

'I hope I haven't interrupted something?' Glenda Howarth said cattily.

Telling Andie that she hoped no such thing at all! The other woman was enjoying herself at the expense of Adam's marriage to Andie—and Andie, for one, had taken enough of it.

'Not in the least, Mrs Howarth,' she came back smoothly. 'Adam and I will have the rest of our lives together, I certainly don't begrudge you a few minutes of his time.' Her emerald-hard gaze told Glenda Howarth that if it amounted to anything more than that, begrudging a few minutes of Adam's time would be the least of the other woman's problems.

Blue eyes returned to hers unflinchingly. 'That's very gracious of you.'

Gracious was the last thing Andie felt—she could cheerfully have wiped that condescending smile off the other woman's face! But, having no idea what this woman meant to Adam, that was something she couldn't do.

She turned to Adam. 'I'll give you a ring later.' She reached up and placed a light kiss on his rigidly clenched jaw. 'Goodbye, Mrs Howarth,' she added with more than a little force.

'Miss Summer.' The other woman was still confidently unperturbed.

Adam seemed stunned by the suddenness of her decision to leave, Andie realised as she turned away from them to

signal a passing taxi to stop. He hadn't come out of that
stupor by the time she had climbed into the waiting taxi
and turned to give him a dismissive wave through the window.

She gave the taxi driver her address before sinking wearily back into the seat, realising as she did so that her legs
were actually shaking.

She hadn't liked Glenda Howarth on sight, and further
acquaintance hadn't changed that opinion, the other woman
proving to be hard and brittle. Worst of all, she seemed to
have some sort of hold over Adam...

That was the thing that bothered Andie the most about
that unexpected meeting.

Adam hadn't been at all pleased earlier when Jonas had
told them Rome had put their marriage announcement in
the newspaper, and at the time Andie had guessed there
was someone that Adam didn't want to see that announcement.

She now knew, with sickening clarity, that person was
Glenda Howarth!

Who was Glenda Howarth?

More to the point, what did the other woman mean to
Adam...?

Andie had a feeling she wouldn't like the answer to either of those questions!

Adam watched Andie as she chatted happily with Danie
across the dinner table.

As promised, Andie had telephoned him at five-thirty to
tell him she had managed to contact Danie, and that the
four of them were meeting up for dinner at Cleo's at eight
o'clock.

Andie had sounded bright and cheerful enough on the
telephone, just as she had looked stunningly beautiful in a

knee-length black dress when he'd called at her apartment for her shortly after seven-thirty so that they could drive to the restaurant together. And she seemed happy enough in Danie and Jonas's company now too.

But for all that bright happiness Andie portrayed, Adam knew that something had subtly changed between them this afternoon. Andie was politely gracious when he told her how beautiful she looked this evening, politely considerate of everything he said, politely distant! In fact, Andie was just too damned *polite*!

He knew the reason for it, of course. Andie was puzzled, if not a little hurt, by that strained meeting with Glenda earlier this afternoon. The problem was, he wasn't sure, without telling Andie everything, how he could make things right between them again. It was something he had hoped to avoid until after he and Andie were safely married.

Although he had had the satisfaction, after Andie had left so abruptly, of leaving Glenda in no doubt that if she tried to interfere in his life again in the way she had today, then she would get nothing else from him. Absolutely nothing.

As Glenda's interest in him had only ever been a financial one, he was pretty sure she would take note of that warning.

Which took care of Glenda, for the immediate future, but did absolutely nothing to put things right between himself and Andie. If he tried to touch her, put his arm about her waist, hold her hand, she found some way of eluding that touch. When he had moved to kiss her on arrival at her apartment earlier, she had turned her face slightly so that he'd ended up kissing her cheek.

In other words, he was back to square one as far as Andie was concerned!

It wasn't acceptable to him! Being with Andie was the best thing that had ever happened in his life—and he wasn't about to lose it.

He reached out and took her hand in his, his grasp tightening as she seemed to instinctively move away. 'Isn't it time you told Danie our news…?' he prompted as Andie turned to look at him questioningly.

Her cheeks became slightly heated, her gaze shifting uncertainly away from his.

Andie didn't want to tell Danie they were expecting twins!

Adam knew that as clearly as if Andie had shouted the words out loud, feeling a sudden sinking feeling in the pit of his stomach. Andie had seemed as excited as he was earlier when Jonas had shown them the two babies on the screen. Obviously it was something that had happened since that had changed that.

Glenda had happened!

His mouth tightened at that realisation. Glenda was responsible for much of the unhappiness in his own life; he would not allow her to be the cause of any in Andie's.

'We already know about the wedding.' Danie was the one to break what was becoming an uncomfortably long silence following Adam's question.

'Andie?' Adam prompted again, his hand tightening reassuringly about Andie's now.

She drew in a sharp breath before smiling across at her sister. Adam just hoped he was the only one who could tell how strained that smile was!

'Jonas did a scan for us today,' Andie told Danie lightly. 'It was—very illuminating,' she added with a return of some of her mischievous humour.

Danie turned to her quietly listening husband. 'You didn't mention that,' she rebuked playfully.

Jonas shrugged. 'Doctor and patient confidentiality still stands, even from the patient's sister. Even if that sister happens to be my own wife. As you very well know.'

'Can you believe this man, Adam?' Danie turned to him, her eyes twinkling humorously. 'For several weeks after Jonas and I first met, I thought he was a heart specialist, or, at worst, a cancer specialist!' She shook her head. 'I even got the patient wrong!'

Adam smiled. 'Sounds like an interesting story,' he said.

He had always rather liked the red-haired Danie; of the three sisters she was probably the most spirited. Although Jonas didn't seem to be having any problems as her husband, looking confidently relaxed as he sat beside his wife.

The other man had a quiet strength of character that was more than a match for Danie's more extrovert one, Adam was quickly learning. The other man was also highly intelligent. Jonas was a very capable obstetrician. And obviously deeply in love with Danie. It was the latter that made Adam like him the most.

'Oh, it is,' Danie confirmed. 'So tell me your news,' she demanded. 'Obviously Jonas already knows it.' She gave her husband a playfully chastising look.

Adam could see that Andie was still having trouble sharing their news. 'How about if we show you instead of telling you?' he suggested, taking out his wallet to remove the photograph Jonas had given him earlier.

Danie's reaction to the two babies was as joyful as expected, the two men sharing an indulgent glance as the two women launched into conversation about twins, baby buggies, cots, clothes, everything that could possibly be needed for the arrival of two babies instead of one.

'I'm afraid this evening must have been very boring for you,' Andie said shyly on the drive back to her apartment later—much later—that evening. 'All that baby talk,' she explained.

Adam raised blond brows, his mouth tight. 'And why should I be bored talking about our babies?'

Andie tensed beside him. 'Most men would be.'

'I'm not most men, Andie,' he returned. 'You should know that by now.'

Two steps forward, and one step back, he inwardly acknowledged. He hoped it wasn't always going to be like this between them.

But Andie hadn't mentioned that earlier meeting with Glenda so far this evening, and Adam was loath to do so earlier. Except that he knew that was what was putting this particular barrier between them.

He drew in some air. 'About Glenda—'

'I don't want to know, Adam,' Andie rebuked him.

'No?' He blinked his surprise.

She gave a decisive shake of her head. 'She's obviously someone from a different part of your life, a life I have no part of, which makes her none of my business, either.' But that slightly emotional quiver to Andie's voice implied she didn't really believe that.

Adam was stunned for a few seconds after this announcement. Andie believed—she thought—Andie believed he had been *involved* with Glenda!

Why should she have thought otherwise? Came the immediate question. To look at, Glenda was a beautiful woman—even if that wasn't true inside! He hadn't offered any explanation about his relationship with Glenda, so what else was Andie to think?

Involved with Glenda?

He would rather be involved with a snake; it would probably be less deadly!

But without telling Andie the truth, he couldn't very well contradict that impression...

'You won't be seeing her again,' he told Andie.

'I don't think that's the point here, Adam—do you?' Andie insisted.

'Then what *is* the point?'

'Whether or not *you'll* be seeing Glenda Howarth again, of course!'

His breath caught, and held, in his throat. Could he make Andie that particular promise, and keep it?

CHAPTER TWELVE

WITHOUT Adam having to say anything, Andie knew she was asking him something he couldn't, in truth, agree to!

Which left the two of them precisely where?

They had agreed there would be no one else in either of their lives, that they were going to give their marriage every chance of success. Adam had agreed to that. In fact, he had insisted on it.

But not where Glenda Howarth was concerned, obviously.

What hold did the other woman have on him? There had to be something. Because there certainly wasn't any love between them; there was no way Andie could forget the contemptuous way Adam had looked at the other woman earlier today.

So why couldn't he agree not to see the other woman again?

If Adam wasn't prepared to tell her that—and by the stubborn set to his mouth, he obviously wasn't!—then she would have to ask someone else.

Glenda Howarth...?

Andie quivered with distaste just at the thought of having to see the other woman again.

Not Glenda Howarth, then.

But someone else. Because there was no way they could have the spectre of Glenda Howarth standing between them when they were married in just over two weeks' time.

'Never mind, Adam,' Andie said sharply. 'You obviously need to give that suggestion some thought.'

'It isn't that—'

'Do you want to come up for a cup of coffee?' she invited as they arrived outside her apartment block, not particularly wanting this evening to end with obvious strain between them. One evening like that had been enough as far as she was concerned.

Adam turned to look at her in the dark confines of the car. 'I would love to—if you're sure you aren't too tired?'

'I had a nap this afternoon,' she explained as she got out of the car. She knew it wasn't a very gracious invitation, but it was the best she could do for the moment.

Adam seemed happy enough with it, anyway, accompanying her up to her apartment, helping her to prepare the coffee in the kitchen before carrying the tray into the sitting-room.

However, that awkward silence fell between them again as they sipped their coffee.

Finally, Adam drew in a heavy breath. 'Andie, I know you don't want to hear about Glenda—'

'I don't,' she agreed.

'Any more than I want to talk about her,' he continued, his expression grim. 'However, I do have one thing to say on the subject...'

Andie briefly closed her eyes, a vision instantly coming to mind of Adam's face this afternoon, as they'd looked at the screen that had shown them their two babies. It had been a face full of love.

She had known Adam most of her life, knew that he was an honourable man. Whatever he chose to tell her about Glenda Howarth, she would believe him.

She opened her eyes, looking across at him. 'Yes?' she pressed gently.

Adam put his coffee-cup down before standing up, coming over to crouch down next to her chair, reaching out to grasp both her hands in one of his. 'I want you to know that Glenda Howarth means nothing to me. Is nothing to me.'

Andie looked at him, could see the worry in his silver gaze, the dark frown to his brow. It was very important to him that she believe him...

She swallowed hard. 'All right, Adam.' She nodded.

'Is it?' His frown was pained now. 'Is it really all right?'

Her expression softened as she saw the raw uncertainty in his face, reaching out a slightly trembling hand to lightly caress the hard curve of his jaw. 'Yes, Adam, it's all right,' she told him, feeling relieved herself at a partial return to the closeness they had known earlier today; she loved Adam too much to be able to stand the desolation of that distance between them!

'God, Andie...!' He reached forward and pulled her into his arms, his face buried in the perfumed silkiness of her hair. 'This evening has been—awful!' he groaned achingly.

She reached up and touched his silver-blond hair. 'I won't tell Danie and Jonas you said so!'

He pulled back slightly to look at her. 'It had nothing to do with Danie and Jonas, and you know it.'

Yes, she knew it. It had been as if there were an invisible barrier between them most of the evening. Even though Andie had known she was responsible for most of it, that she'd flinched away from Adam every time he'd touched her, she hadn't seemed to be able to do anything about it. But she had hated that distance between them as much as Adam obviously had.

Adam's hands cradled either side of her face. 'I will never do anything that might put my relationship with you and our children at risk,' he promised her.

Tears suddenly glistened in her eyes. Their children....

It all still seemed somehow like a dream. A wonderful dream, but a dream nevertheless.

Adam bent his head, kissing her gently on the lips, sipping and tasting their sweetness, until Andie gave a low groan in her throat and deepened the kiss, her arms moving up about his shoulders as she pressed herself against him.

She loved this man, loved him so deeply, that she knew in her heart that she would forgive him anything.

'Andie...?' Adam raised his head to look down at her with needy grey eyes.

She wanted him, needed him, loved him. There was nothing else.

'Adam!' she breathed, heated colour in her cheeks as she knew she wanted him more than she had ever wanted anything in her life.

He looked at her searchingly for several long seconds before standing up to bend down and sweep her up into his arms.

'I'm too heavy for you,' she protested, at the same time clinging tightly around his neck.

He grinned down at her. 'Maybe in a couple of months or so, you might be!' he conceded. 'At the moment you're still as light as air.'

'Where are we going?' she asked as he strode across the room.

'Wonderful as it might have been the first time, I don't think we should make love on the floor a second time!' He softly kicked open the door that led to her bedroom, pulling back the bedclothes to gently lay her down on top of the bed, before joining her there.

Andie turned into his arms, a bedside lamp their only illumination as they gazed hungrily at each other. She would never have believed, at the beginning of this evening, that the two of them would be here together like this!

She reached up to curl her fingers into the thick blondness of his hair, loving the silky feel of it, suddenly feeling slightly shy. What if that one time together had been a fluke? What if this time it all went—?

Adam laughed softly as he gazed indulgently down at her. 'Have a little faith, Andie,' he chided affectionately.

As he began to kiss her, her body suddenly alive with a hundred senses, her mind went completely blank, and there was only feeling left, vein-tingling, spine-thrilling sensation.

Adam's hands roamed restlessly down the length of her body, even as his lips trailed an erotic pattern down the creamy column of her throat to the hollows below, the curve of her breasts visible above the rounded neckline of the black dress she wore.

'You are so beautiful, Andie.' The warmth of his breath caressed her heated skin as he slid the zip down the back of her dress. 'So incredibly beautiful.'

It was impossible to feel in the least self-conscious in the face of such warm admiration, her dress completely discarded now, only black lace bra and matching panties covering her nakedness.

'Let me,' she said, reaching up to unbutton his shirt, smoothing the material back to run her hands caressingly over the smoothness of his skin, fingertips tingling over the silky hair that covered his chest.

There had seemed no opportunity, the last time they'd been together like this, to actually touch and feel, to learn the contours of each other's body.

Adam's body was lean and hard, his legs long and muscular, skin lightly tanned—obviously not all of his time was spent behind a desk, on the telephone, or on a plane!—and covered with fine silver-blonde hair.

As he pulled her in tightly against his body, only thin

garments still between them, Andie could feel the hard evidence of his desire.

She moved sensuously against him, her senses raised to fever pitch, her eyes deeply green as she looked up at him pleadingly. She wanted more—so much more!—wanted to be completely naked against him, wanted—

'Not until we're married—remember?' Once again Adam seemed able to read her thoughts, regret in his voice.

She shook her head, reaching out to caress him. 'That doesn't seem important any more.'

'It is to me,' he told her firmly, his hand tightly gripping her wrist.

But as if to take any sting out of his words, his head lowered, lips closing hotly over one bra-covered nipple, sucking the sensitive tip into the moist cavern of his mouth.

Andie's head went back, her eyes closing as she groaned low in her throat, her body feeling on fire as Adam released her hand to caress her other breast, heated pleasure now coursing through her body.

Her breathing was short and shallow as she felt the sensations building up inside her, sure that she was going to completely explode as she felt Adam's caress against her panties.

Waves of pleasure washed over her with ever-increasing pressure, until she felt as if she couldn't stand any more, her body arching in aching ecstasy.

The aftermath of that pleasure left her weak and exhausted, lying limply in Adam's arms now.

He raised his head to look at her as she still trembled in his arms. 'Are you all right? I didn't hurt you?'

If that was hurting—!

'No, you didn't hurt me,' she assured him, knowing that Adam had taken her to the plateau of complete pleasure. 'Although I did feel as if I had died and gone to heaven.'

Adam laughed huskily, smoothing back the blonde tangle of her hair from the heat of her face. 'That's how I hoped you would feel!' He reached beneath them to pull the bed-clothes up over both of them. 'And now I would like a pleasure that was denied me last time,' he said.

She looked up at him, unsure of what he meant. She was pregnant as a result of their last lovemaking, so what—?

He looked down at her with laughing grey eyes. 'The pleasure of having you fall asleep in my arms,' he explained with playful rebuke.

Andie stared at him in the glow from the bedside lamp. 'But—'

'Sleep, woman,' he commanded, his arm about her as he put her head on his shoulder before reaching out to turn off the lamp.

Andie lay beside him in the darkness. But he hadn't— He had given her pleasure, and yet he—

'We have the rest of our lives, Andie,' he murmured beside her in the darkness as he sensed her troubled thoughts. 'Tonight I wanted to give you pleasure.'

And he had.

He certainly had!

Complete. Utterly. Unselfishly…!

'Will you stop pacing up and down on the same piece of carpet, Adam? You'll wear it out!'

He paused to give Rome a glowering glare. But he changed the direction of his pacing, nonetheless.

He had known, after that meeting with Glenda yesterday, Andie's reaction to it, that he had to talk to someone. Unfortunately, the person he was closest to in the world—apart from Andie, herself!—was Rome. Who, of course, also happened to be Andie's father!

Which explained why he was pacing impatiently up and

down the sitting-room at the estate house. He had no idea how to even begin telling Rome about Glenda!

Rome sighed. 'Is this going to take long, Adam? Because I have a wedding of my own to go to next week, you know!' he added satirically, perfectly relaxed as he sat in one of the armchairs watching Adam.

'Very funny!' Adam grimaced.

'I doubt Audrey would share that sentiment if I failed to appear at the church simply because it took you a week to get round to what you want to say!' Rome drawled.

Adam stopped his pacing. 'It's all very difficult...'

Rome looked concerned. 'You aren't thinking of letting Andie down, are you?' He spoke mildly enough, but there was a definite edge to his tone as he looked far from relaxed now.

'Don't be ridiculous,' Adam came back impatiently.

'That's okay, then.' The older man settled back into his chair. 'Because you would seriously be stretching the bounds of our friendship if you were to even consider doing that.'

'I've just said I'm not,' Adam snapped irritably.

'I heard you. Just as I heard you the day you came here to explain to me that you and Andie had been secretly involved with each other for months, and that you were the father of her baby,' Rome continued softly, blue eyes narrowed now.

Adam looked at the other man warily. 'It's true, I am. And by the way, it's babies. Plural,' he added.

Rome gave an abrupt nod of his head. 'Andie came to see me this morning to tell me the good news.'

Andie had been here this morning...?

Adam had left her apartment shortly after eight o'clock this morning, the two of them sharing a pot of coffee before he'd gone back to his own apartment to shower and change ready for going to his office.

Except that he hadn't gone to his office, had spent the morning at his apartment thinking over what he should do about Glenda, finally telephoning Rome and asking if he could come and talk to him.

But Andie had already been here today.

Why? Oh, obviously she would want to tell her father about the twins, but even so...

Adam frowned. 'I didn't realise that.'

Rome shrugged. 'There's no reason why you should have done. I'm pleased for both of you, of course.'

But.

The other man hadn't actually said that, but it was there in the tone of his voice.

Adam also questioned why Rome hadn't told him he knew about the twins when he'd arrived a short time ago. Surely it would have been the most natural thing in the world for Rome to have talked excitedly of the fact that he was now expecting two grandchildren and not one?

Rome stood up. 'I said I heard you last week, Adam— that doesn't mean I believed you. Most people who meet me for the first time believe—as they are supposed to!— that I am just an easygoing man who happened to make a couple of lucky business decisions early on in my career, and that I have built on those decisions because of that earlier success. That's most people, Adam,' he repeated. 'I didn't count you amongst their number!'

He had told Andie only yesterday that he wasn't most men!

But he knew that wasn't what Rome meant at all. Rome was right; Adam had never been fooled by that happy-go-lucky philanthropic guise Rome wore for the general public. Rome had achieved his success by shrewd intelligence, accompanied by kid-glove ruthlessness.

'Audrey told me I should leave the subject alone,' Rome continued. 'And while I accede to my future wife's views on most subjects—' he smiled tightly '—Andie's future happiness is not something I intend letting anyone play around with.'

He looked across at Adam with narrowed blue eyes, the two men of similar height and build, the fourteen years' difference in their ages noticeable only in the lines of experience beside Rome's eyes and mouth. But it was a difference Adam had always known he should be wary of...

'I am as concerned for Andie's future happiness as you are,' Adam told him shortly.

'Are you?' Rome returned in measured tones. 'Then let me tell you that I was never fooled for a moment by that story of the two of you keeping your relationship a secret. Not one single minute, Adam,' he repeated firmly as Adam would have spoken. 'My daughters were simply not brought up to be secretive,' he declared with proud affection. 'However,' he went on, 'at the time, I considered the details of your earlier involvement none of my business.'

'"At the time"...?' Adam echoed.

Rome nodded abruptly. 'I'm still not going to pry, Adam; the two of you have decided to marry, and that is the end of the matter as far as I'm concerned.'

There was still a but. Adam sensed it.

'However,' Rome said, 'Andie's visit here this morning changed things somewhat.'

'It did?' Again Adam looked at the other man warily. This wasn't turning out at all as he had imagined it would!

Rome gave a stiff inclination of his head. 'My daughter is under the impression that there's a—complication in your life that may affect your married life together.'

Adam drew in a harsh breath. He had come here for the very reason of talking to Rome about that complication. But now he felt on the defensive.

He moistened dry lips. 'Did she tell you what that complication was?'

Rome gave a humourless smile. 'As it happens, yes, she did. But she didn't need to. I already knew.'

Adam stared at him dazedly. Rome knew? But how——? The only person he had ever told about Glenda had been Barbara, and he couldn't believe——

Rome softly broke into his racing thoughts. 'Adam, when you came to me twenty years ago with your business proposal, I was a man of thirty-four, with a wife and very young family; I took risks, but I wasn't stupid. I had your background thoroughly checked out before I agreed to finance you.'

Adam could only stare at the other man. Rome really did know! All this time he had known—and never said anything!

Rome gave an impatient sigh, moving over to the drinks tray to pour them both a glass of brandy, handing Adam one of those glasses before sipping at his own.

'What are you so afraid of, Adam?' Rome looked at him over the rim of his glass.

Losing Andie! He was so close, so close to having her for all time, and the thought of losing her now——!

Rome briefly closed his eyes. 'Do you have so little faith in Andie that you think she won't want to marry you once she knows about your past?'

Adam swallowed hard, dropping down heavily into a chair. 'You don't understand,' he groaned. 'Andie doesn't love me. And once she knows—'

'Andie doesn't love you!' Rome repeated with incredulous disbelief. 'Are you stupid, Adam? Or just blind? Andie has worshipped the ground you walked on since she was seven years old!'

Adam took a gulp of the brandy. 'You're wrong. She—'

'Take my word for it, Adam,' the older man broke in. 'Andie loves you. She always has.'

Adam looked across at him. Could Rome possibly be right? Did Andie care for him?

No! He couldn't believe that. He didn't dare take the risk of believing that.

'Adam, this morning I told Andie that if she had any doubts, if she had changed her mind about marrying you, that it was all right with me,' Rome told him gruffly. 'That I would stand by whatever decision she made.'

Adam's breath caught and held in his throat. 'And?' he finally gasped weakly.

Rome smiled. 'She told me that if she didn't marry you she would never marry anyone—'

'That's because of the babies—'

'No, it isn't, damn it!' Rome rasped harshly, blue eyes blazing. 'Adam, I know how difficult it's been for you,' he continued more gently. 'But you aren't responsible for your past. You were a child—'

Adam's eyes clouded. 'Don't you see? My past makes me the man I am!'

Rome sighed. 'I accept that, unlike my own children, you were brought up in a world that didn't have any affection, let alone love. I can even understand how it must be difficult for you now to accept having someone love you. But the Summer family have always loved you. And Andie more than all of us.'

Was Rome right? Was he just unable to believe that anyone could love him?

Could Andie ever love him...? Was Rome right, and she already did love him?

He thought back over the last couple of weeks, their initial awkwardness together, and the closeness they had known last night...

He looked across at Rome, only to find the other man looking right back at him, his gaze steadily challenging. 'What else did Andie say to you this morning?'

The other man hesitated. 'As you might suppose, she asked me if I knew anything about a woman called Glenda Howarth.'

Adam tensed. 'And?'

'I had to answer her honestly and say no,' Rome came back easily.

'But—'

'Adam, I would never lie to Andie,' Rome assured him. 'I have never lied to any of my children, and I'm not about to start now. The truth is I don't know anything about Glenda Howarth. Glenda Munroe is another matter, however. But that isn't what Andie asked me.'

Glenda Munroe...

Yes, that had once been her name. The same surname as his. Before she'd remarried.

'I also happen to believe, Adam,' Rome said, 'that it is for you to tell Andie about the past. About Glenda.'

It was. He knew it was.

He was just so terrified of losing Andie when he had done so, of her pity, if not her disgust.

Despite Rome's assurances that Andie loved him...

CHAPTER THIRTEEN

ANDIE watched Adam as he walked restlessly up and down her sitting-room.

He looked terrible, his face pale, a grimness about his eyes and mouth that she had never seen there before.

She had no idea why. Last night, sleeping in each other's arms, had been wonderful. As had sitting drinking coffee together this morning before he'd left.

But Adam had telephoned her late this afternoon and suggested he come over to her apartment this evening, turning down her offer to cook them both dinner. Andie had an idea why that was now; Adam didn't look as if he would be staying long enough to eat dinner!

Finally she could stand the silence no longer. 'Adam—'

'Andie, I have something to tell you,' he burst out. 'It isn't something I'm going to enjoy telling you, but I know it has to be done.'

Glenda Howarth...?

Surely it had to be something to do with the other woman; Adam had changed since that meeting with Glenda Howarth outside his office yesterday.

Andie had been to see her father this morning, in the hope that he might be able to shed some light on the other woman's role in Adam's life; after all, the men had been close friends for years. But Rome had been less than helpful, his expression completely blank at the mention of the other woman's name. Although he had promised to see what he could find out about her.

But from the expression on Adam's face, Rome wouldn't

173

need to bother; Adam was going to tell her about the other woman himself.

She moistened suddenly dry lips. Adam looked so unhappy about all this that she just knew it was going to be awful.

But what on earth could be so terrible about his relationship with Glenda Howarth that it made him look like this? Andie had given a lot of thought to the other woman today—and the only thing she had been able to come up with, the very worst scenario, was that Adam had once been married to Glenda Howarth. After all, she knew little or nothing about his life before twenty years ago.

But even so, such a young marriage, a marriage that must have gone terribly wrong to have ended before Adam was even twenty, would have no significance in his life now.

Not that Andie would like the idea of Adam ever having been married to anyone else—and especially a woman like Glenda Howarth, a woman she had disliked on sight!—but it wasn't so terrible that Adam had to be reluctant to tell her about it. Was it...?

Or perhaps she had it all wrong, and Adam wasn't going to tell her something awful about Glenda Howarth, perhaps he was going to tell her of his feelings for her mother. That, she most certainly did not want to hear!

She stood up. 'Do I really need to hear this, Adam? Is it going to help anything?' she reasoned.

He gave a slightly bitter smile. 'Probably not,' he conceded. 'In fact, I'm sure not. But Rome has convinced me it isn't something you should learn about after we're married.'

'Rome has?' Her eyes widened. When had Adam spoken to her father about this? Before or after her own visit this morning? How had Rome reacted to being told that Adam had been in love with Barbara all these years?

Adam went on with his explanation. 'He doesn't believe it would be fair to you not to tell you before we're married. And after thinking about it, I know he's right,' he acknowledged.

Fair to her? Had it been fair to Rome, even if he were finding happiness a second time in marrying Audrey, to burden him with the truth of Adam's feelings towards Barbara?

'How did my father react?' she asked worriedly. After all, such knowledge was sure to put a strain on Rome and Adam's friendship. That was the last thing any of them needed just now!

Adam sighed. 'Apparently, he already knew.'

Well, she had guessed that much, her father was far from stupid. But actually hearing the words must have made it seem so much worse.

Andie was puzzled. 'I don't know what you hoped to achieve by talking to my father about this.' Any more than he expected to achieve anything positive by telling her either! It might succeed in easing Adam's conscience, but it certainly wouldn't do anything to help their own marriage.

'I didn't hope to achieve anything,' Adam protested. 'I just needed someone to talk to, and Rome was the only person I could think of. It helped that he already knew.'

'I'm sure it did,' Andie snapped.

'He mentioned that you had been to see him this morning, too.' Adam looked at her searchingly.

'That was about something else completely,' she dismissed impatiently.

Adam frowned. 'I don't think so...'

Andie was becoming more and more confused the longer this conversation continued along these abstract lines. 'Maybe if you just say what you feel you have to say,

Adam…?' she prompted, anxious to get this over with now, her nerves already strung out to breaking-point.

He gave another deep sigh. 'It's been buried inside me for so long—! Would you like to sit down again?' he invited.

Maybe she had better; she didn't want to fall down!

'There,' she told him once she was back in her chair, looking up at him expectantly.

'Right. Well. To start at the beginning, we have to go back thirty-five years—'

'Thirty-five years?' Andie echoed incredulously. 'But you would only have been four at the time!'

'Yes,' he agreed, no longer looking at her, no longer looking at anything it seemed, his expression blank, his thoughts all inwards.

If this thing—whatever it was—went back to when Adam was four, then this couldn't possibly be anything to do with her mother. Or Glenda Howarth either, that Andie could see…?

'I was four,' Adam confirmed gruffly. 'And so was my—my brother. Harry.'

Andie had never known he had a brother, let alone—

Twins! If Adam and Harry had both been four, then that meant they had to be twins. The twin connection in Adam's family that he had told her about.

But where was Harry now?

Adam looked at her with pained eyes. 'Harry is dead.'

Andie's gasp of dismay caught and held in her throat at Adam's next comment.

'And I killed him.'

She stared across at him with incredulous green eyes. He couldn't have just said— He had been four years old, for goodness' sake!

'Oh, not with my own bare hands,' Adam assured her bitterly. 'But I was still responsible for his death.'

Andie swallowed hard, shaking her head. 'I'm not sure a four-year-old has enough awareness of life to be held responsible for anything, let alone—let alone—Adam—'

'No, don't touch me!' he instructed harshly as she would have stood up and gone to him.

Andie subsided back into her chair. But only because he'd asked her to. What she most wanted to do was cradle him in her arms while he told her the rest of what he felt he had to say.

Adam turned away, swallowing convulsively. 'Harry was my identical twin to look at, but we were completely different in personality. I was the extrovert, the outgoing one. Harry was shy, liked to sit quietly looking at books. But at the same time, he would always follow where I led. My mother—our mother,' he amended, 'was twenty when we were born. We never knew our father. They were married, but he—he walked out when he found out they were expecting twins. Too much responsibility, I suppose.' Adam took a gulp of air. 'By the time we were six months old our mother had begun to go out in the evenings. She couldn't afford to pay for babysitters,' he added bitterly as Andie would have spoken. 'By the time we were three, she was out almost every night. I was left in charge, because I was the oldest—'

'By how much?' Andie gasped, horrified at what he was telling her. She had read about things like this in the newspapers, of course, but had never guessed that this could be Adam's childhood.

'Five minutes,' Adam answered flatly. 'Anyway, one night, when we were four, our mother had gone out as usual, and—the money ran out in the electricity meter.' He moistened dry lips. 'I couldn't find any money to put in it, so I—I lit a candle in our bedroom. Harry had never liked the dark, and I—I fell asleep!' he continued emotionally. 'The candle must have fallen over, caught the curtains alight, and within minutes the place was an inferno. I couldn't find Harry amongst the smoke! I looked and I looked, but I couldn't find him. Then a neighbour burst in and carried me out. I never saw Harry again.'

Andie's sob caught in her throat. How horrible. How absolutely, heartbreakingly horrible. For Adam.

'By the time my mother returned from her evening out, our apartment was burnt beyond recognition. And Harry was dead,' Adam said numbly.

A sudden—shocking!—truth hit Andie like a lightning bolt. Glenda Howarth, still beautiful but older than she actually looked, was Adam's mother!

Andie didn't know how she knew, couldn't even have said where the idea had come from. But she knew it with blinding certainty.

Andie stood up, determined to go to Adam now whether he wanted her to or not, putting her hand tentatively on the rigidness of his arm. 'Glenda Howarth is your mother, isn't she, Adam?' Andie said evenly.

His mouth twisted with distaste. 'She is,' he confirmed. 'And I've hated her from the day Harry died.'

Andie felt choked. She understood his feelings, even while she ached with the pain he must have suffered at his twin's death.

She also understood now why he was so determined to be a good and loving father to his own children. Even if he couldn't love their mother, he would love and take care of his children.

Adam looked searchingly at Andie. He knew she was tender-hearted enough to empathise with his trauma at

Harry's death. It was his mother that was the real skeleton in his cupboard. After all that had happened, all the years of hating her, she was still his mother. Much as he hated it, her blood ran in his veins.

He had decided very early in his life that he would never love anyone again. When his mother had come back into his life fifteen years ago, he had known it was the right decision; how could he ever offer any woman Glenda as a mother-in-law? Certainly not Andie, who had only ever known love and sunshine in her own life.

He grasped Andie's arms now, putting her firmly away from him, still not sure how this conversation was going to turn out. 'It was so hard for me to believe Harry was really gone. He was the other half of myself.' His expression softened. 'You would have liked him, Andie—'

'Don't!' she choked, tears glistening on her lashes.

'No,' he accepted heavily. 'It doesn't help, does it? I go to his grave sometimes, talk to him, but that doesn't help, either.' He swallowed hard.

'I'll come with you next time,' Andie told him huskily. 'We can tell him about our own twins. He would probably like that.'

She understood that, at least! He had hoped that she would, but been so afraid that she wouldn't...!

'It's been so long since I was able to share Harry with anyone,' he admitted, his own throat choked with tears. 'Your mother understood, but—'

'My mother?' Andie repeated. 'She knew about all this?'

'I told her,' he admitted, sensing a sudden distance widening between Andie and himself. A distance he didn't understand. 'Your mother was one of the most beautiful people I have ever known, gave me back my belief in human love and kindness, a belief that had been missing from my life for so many years—'

'Adam, I don't want to hear how you felt about my mother!' Andie protested emotionally.

He blinked his surprise at her vehemence. 'But—'

'If we're to stand any chance of building a future together, Adam—and I believe from this conversation that you still want that—then it has to be with no emotional baggage,' Andie told him firmly. 'Oh, I don't mean Harry,' she assured pleadingly at his pained frown. 'Losing Harry, an identical twin, must have been like losing half of yourself.'

'Worse,' he confirmed bleakly. 'We were so close we could finish each other's sentences, read each other's minds. After Harry died I completely withdrew into myself, refused to speak. To anyone. There was an inquest on Harry's death, of course, a social services report on my mother.' He looked steadily at Andie. 'The report showed that my mother's evenings out were spent with a number of different men. Men who gave her money.'

He watched as the truth dawned on Andie, the absolute horror on her face.

His mother, selfish, irresponsible, totally incapable of caring for anyone but herself, had been little better than a prostitute!

Oh, no one had actually used that word at the time, and Adam wouldn't have understood what it meant if they had, but he hadn't even been in his teens when he had worked out for himself that was what his mother had actually been. There was no denying the fact that the men his mother had seen had been on a regular basis, but the plain truth of the matter was, his mother had taken money from those men. Which made her only one thing in his eyes.

In Andie's eyes too...?

This was what he had dreaded Andie finding out: the horrible truth about his mother...

He was unable to look at Andie now. Frightened of what he might see in her face!

'The authorities decided that Glenda wasn't a fit mother to look after me. But with typical selfishness, my mother refused to even think of agreeing to adoption, so I was put into care—'

'No!' Andie protested brokenly.

He gave a humourless smile. 'It was the best thing anyone could have done for me. Away from her, from the place where Harry and I had known such unhappiness, I at last began to respond to people, to talk again. On the few occasions when my mother came to visit I refused to see her. Her birthday and Christmas presents were always sent back unopened, until she finally stopped sending them.' He at last explained the lack of them in his childhood; it had been an act of deliberate denial on his part! 'In fact, I didn't see her again until I was twenty-five or so. When I had begun to make a name for myself—and obviously money, too!— as a film producer,' he explained bitterly.

'After all that had happened, she came to you and asked for money?' Andie gasped disbelievingly.

He still clearly remembered that first meeting with Glenda after twenty years of inwardly denying she had ever existed. She had looked exactly the same, still beautiful— and still the same selfishly grasping woman she had always been.

He nodded. 'That was when I talked to your mother about her. I had to tell someone.' He had hated Glenda. But at the same time, she was his mother, his only living relative, and those two emotions had been at war inside him.

'Adam—'

'Andie, I don't understand this problem with your mother?' he protested. 'She's the one who helped me to see the past objectively, helped me to understand that no one is all black, just as no one is all white. My mother had been barely twenty when we were born, abandoned by her husband, left alone with two babies to bring up as best she could. Barbara never tried to excuse Glenda's behaviour, but she did at least succeed in helping me to pity her,' he recalled heavily.

'You loved my mother!' Andie burst out forcefully.

'Well, of course I loved her,' he confirmed. Barbara had helped him retain his sanity fifteen years ago when Glenda, recently divorced from her second husband, had suddenly appeared back in his life. Without Barbara's gentle guidance his reaction to Glenda might have been completely different! 'How could I help but love her?' He shook his head. 'Barbara was everything a mother should be: loving, caring, giving. Everything my own mother wasn't, and never could be!'

Andie was very pale now, eyes hugely green against that paleness. 'She was also another man's wife!'

'Well, of course she—' Adam broke off his exclamation, suddenly still as he looked searchingly down at Andie. She returned that gaze unflinchingly, but once again there were tears glistening in her eyes. 'Andie, I loved Barbara like the mother I had never had, the mother I never would have.' He firmly grasped the tops of her arms. 'And Barbara being the woman she was, she took me in as if I were one of her own children.'

'How could she possibly seem like a mother to you?'' Andie scorned in a pained voice. 'She was only twelve years older than you!'

'Andie—' He paused disbelievingly. 'Tell me if I'm understanding this correctly; do you believe I was in love with your mother…?'

She raised her chin proudly. 'And weren't you?'

'Good God, no,' he answered unhesitantly, shaking his head dazedly. 'I told you, she was like a mother to me, gave me the gentleness and love, the acceptance for who and what I am, that had been missing from my life for so long. Rome instinctively understood that. I always thought you girls did, too,' he said. 'Obviously I was wrong…'

Very, very wrong, if Andie had believed all this time that he was in love with her mother!

But if Andie believed that, had always believed that, why had she agreed to marry him? He couldn't believe it was just the pregnancy.

Hope began to burn deep inside him as he looked at Andie's palely intense face. Hope that perhaps Rome had been right about Andie's feelings towards him, after all…?

He knew that he was about to take the biggest risk of his life, bigger even than telling Andie the truth about his mother. But if he and Andie were ever to know any happiness together, it was a risk he had to take.

'Andie,' he began shakily, 'there's a very good reason why I was never in love with your mother…' He paused, clenching his hands at his sides so that she shouldn't see the way they were trembling. 'And that reason is because I'm very much in love with someone else. And have been for more years than I care to think about.'

Andie's throat moved convulsively. 'Do you really think I want to hear this?' she cried emotionally. 'We're supposed to be marrying each other in two weeks' time!'

'Do you still want to go ahead with that? Now that I've told you about my own childhood? My mother,' he asked hardly. 'You won't be seeing her again, by the way,' he continued grimly. 'That last meeting with her was exactly that.' He had told Glenda in no uncertain terms exactly what he thought of her, what he had always thought of her. As Barbara had told him he would feel strong enough to do one day. He did not want Glenda anywhere near Andie or their two children.

'You aren't your mother, Adam—'

'Her blood runs in my veins!' he bit out.

Andie gave a shake of her head. 'You were practically a baby the last time you lived with her. And I've known you most of my life, Adam, don't believe there is a single part of her in you. You're good, and kind, and—'

'So much in love with you it hurts!' he groaned, giving a self-deprecating laugh as her eyes widened disbelievingly. 'I decided years ago that I would never love anyone again, never need anyone again; Harry had died, my mother had never done a single thing to deserve that title—' He broke off, nervous at going on with this.

But he had started now, he had to go on!

'Over the years, as I worked to build up my company, I convinced myself that was what I was doing, why there was never anyone permanent in my life. It wasn't until your eighteenth birthday that I realised I had only been deluding myself, that there was a much simpler explanation as to why I had never been seriously involved with anyone. Do you remember your eighteenth birthday, Andie?' He looked at her intently.

Andie was still staring up at him, but it was impossible to tell by her dazed expression whether she was merely still disbelieving or just reluctant to hear what he had to say.

'You didn't like the red dress I was wearing,' she finally answered.

He gave a snort. 'I *loved* the red dress you were wearing!' he corrected. 'It was the thought of any other man seeing you in that dress that made me so damned insulting to you that night. I suddenly realised you were no longer a child but a beautiful woman—and that other men would think so too. I also realised,' he continued, 'that I was in love with you. Completely, head over heels, for ever, in love with you.'

Andie blinked. 'You were so horrible to me that night...'

He gave a grimace. 'You would have been horrible too if you had just seen all your carefully laid plans for a carefree bachelor life disappear at the sight of you in a red dress!'

'But I—you—you never said anything! Adam, in all these years you have never given any indication—'

'Andie, you're fourteen years younger than me.' He sighed. 'You had the perfect childhood, a wonderful family, a university degree, a successful career; what did I ever have to offer you—?'

'Yourself!' she cut in emotionally. 'My childhood was perfect,' she acknowledged. 'My family is wonderful. The degree was Rome's idea. My career—for the last five years my career has taken the place of what I really wanted in life!'

Adam tensed. 'And that is?' He held his breath, almost afraid of her answer.

Andie moved towards him, putting her arms about his waist, resting her head against his chest. 'What I have now,' she told him gruffly. 'You. Children. Marriage. Slightly out of the normal order of things,' she acknowledged with a small laugh. 'But I would have settled for just you!'

It was incredible that Andie loved him, too.

Amazing.

But as he gathered her possessively close to him, held her tightly against him, he knew that he accepted that love with open arms, that he worshipped this woman, with every particle of his being.

That he always would.

EPILOGUE

'DO YOU think we will ever get them back?'

Andie followed Adam's amused gaze to watch her family as they oohed and aahed the two babies they held, one in Harrie's arms, the other in Danie's, their two husbands standing beside them smiling indulgently, Rome and Audrey already protesting the two sisters had already held the babies long enough, that as the doting grandparents it was their turn now.

'Eventually.' Andie chuckled, stretching with satisfaction as she turned back to look at Adam.

Her husband.

The love of her life.

As she was his.

She still had to pinch herself occasionally to make sure that she wasn't dreaming, that all the misunderstandings were really over, that she and Adam loved each other.

Even more so since the twins had been born yesterday. She hadn't believed they could possibly be any happier than they already were, their marriage turning out to be everything, and more, that she could ever have hoped for. But as they had shared the experience of their children's birth, held their two tiny sons in their arms, she knew she had been wrong. This was total bliss.

'Although I'm afraid Harry and Peter are going to end up being very spoilt,' she murmured unworriedly.

The names, two boys' and two girls', had been chosen long before the birth. But Andie was inwardly ecstatic that Adam now had another Harry in his life. It could never make up for the loss of the first one, nothing could ever do that, but it was a fitting tribute to the brother Adam had loved so much.

Adam reached out and took one of her hands into his, the love he no longer took pains to hide blazing brightly in his eyes. 'Did I remember to thank you?' he asked.

'For the twins?' She laughed softly. 'I believe we have each other to thank for them!'

Adam shook his head. 'Not for the twins—although God knows I already love them so much I ache with it,' he admitted. 'But it isn't them I thank you for. It's the wonderful family you have given me for them. I—I always wanted—I never believed—'

'They are your family too, Adam.' She squeezed his hand tightly in understanding. They hadn't seen Glenda since that day at Adam's office, never spoke of her, and Andie knew that was the way Adam wanted it to remain. 'They can't love you as much as I do,' she told him. 'But almost!'

As Rome and Audrey finally returned their two sons to them, one in Andie's arms, one in Adam's, the two of them still looking at each other over the babies' heads, and she knew that love would only grow over the years, grow and deepen.

It was for ever.

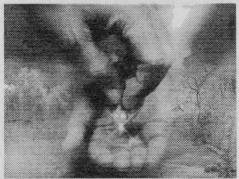
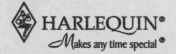

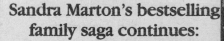

If you enjoyed what you just read,
then we've got an offer you can't resist!

Take 2 bestselling love stories FREE!

Plus get a FREE surprise gift!

Lindsay Armstrong...
Helen Bianchin...
Emma Darcy...
Miranda Lee...

Some of our bestselling writers are Australians!

Look out for their novels about the Wonder from Down Under—where spirited women win the hearts of Australia's most eligible men.

Coming soon:
A QUESTION OF MARRIAGE
by Lindsay Armstrong
On sale October 2001, Harlequin Presents® #2208

And look out for:
FUGITIVE BRIDE
by Miranda Lee
On sale November 2001, Harlequin Presents® #2212

Available wherever Harlequin books are sold.

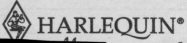

HARLEQUIN®

...ny time special ®

...arlequin.com   HPSEAUS